"What do you want?" Hannah asked

Win's eyes darkened and she stopped breathing. *Stupid question, Hannah. Stupid, stupid.* His answer was obvious in the heat of his gaze, the tenseness of his body.

What he wanted was her.

Just as she wanted him.

Their physical attraction was a fact between them—unpleasant, distracting, constant. And just as there was nothing they could do about the three-hundred-year-old family feud, there was nothing they could do about the primitive longing that had erupted between them.

Well, Hannah thought, there *was* something....

It's no accident that **Carla Neggers** started writing a book last year involving a woman accused of witchcraft. When she learned that 1992 was the 300th anniversary of the Salem witch trials, Carla was inspired. In *Bewitching,* the determined heroine, Hannah Marsh, sets out for Boston to prove that her ancestor was not a witch. It's also no accident that Carla has Hannah stay in a Beacon Hill apartment. Although the cramped basement flat described in the book may not seem like the ideal setting for a romance, Carla would beg to differ. It's modeled after the apartment where she and her husband lived when they were first married. Read on to find out how the bewitching heroine casts a spell over her hero.

BEWITCHING

CARLA NEGGERS

Harlequin Books

TORONTO • NEW YORK • LONDON
AMSTERDAM • PARIS • SYDNEY • HAMBURG
STOCKHOLM • ATHENS • TOKYO • MILAN
MADRID • WARSAW • BUDAPEST • AUCKLAND

Published July 1993

ISBN 0-373-25552-7

BEWITCHING

1

THE PINKS AND ORANGES of dawn sparkled on the bay beyond Marsh Point, off a stretch of southern Maine that was still quiet, still undiscovered by tourists. Hannah Marsh stood on a boulder above the rocky coastline. The wind blew raw and cold, although the calendar said spring had arrived. In defiance of the weather, daffodils bloomed in the little garden outside her cottage.

In Boston the tulips would be out, perhaps even a few leaves budded. It wouldn't be so bad.

"You're going," a gruff voice said behind her.

She turned and smiled at Thackeray Marsh, aged seventy-nine, owner of Marsh Point, fellow historian and her cousin several times removed. He was a stout, fair-skinned, fair-haired man, although not as fair as herself, and kept in shape with dawn and dusk walks along a loop-shaped route that took in most of Marsh Point.

"I have no choice," Hannah said. "Most of the documents I need to examine are in Boston, and anything new on Priscilla Marsh will be there. It's where she lived and died, Thackeray. I have to go."

He snorted. "The Harlings catch you, they'll string you up."

"You said yourself there's only one Harling left in Boston, and he's even older than you are. I'll be fine."

Her elderly cousin squinted his emerald eyes at her. He was wearing an old tweed jacket patched at the elbows and rubber boots that had to be older than she was. His frugality, Hannah had learned in her five years in Maine, was legendary in the region.

"The Harlings and the Marshes haven't had much of anything to do with each other in a hundred years," he said. "Why rock the boat?"

"I'm not rocking the boat. I'm going on a perfectly ordinary, honorable research expedition." She tried not to sound defensive or impatient, but she had gone over her position—over and over it—with Cousin Thackeray. "It's not as if Priscilla Marsh died yesterday, you know."

Judge Cotton Harling had sentenced Priscilla Marsh to death by hanging three hundred years ago. Hannah hoped to have her biography of her ancestor in bookstores by the tricentennial of the execution. Not only would it be good business, but it would pay a nice tribute to a woman who had defied the restrictions of Puritan America—of the Harlings of Boston.

And paid the price, of course. Hannah couldn't forget that.

The wind picked up, and she hugged her oversize sweatshirt closer to her body. Her long, fine, straight blond hair was, fortunately, held back in a hastily tied ponytail. Otherwise it would have tangled badly. Cousin Thackeray barely seemed to notice the cold.

"Hannah, the Harlings resent that we won't let them forget it was a Harling who had Priscilla hanged. We, of course, say they *shouldn't* ever forget. The feud has been going on like this for three hundred years."

She refused to let his dark mood dampen her enthusiasm for what was, after all, a necessary trip—and no doubt would prove boring and routine, involving nothing more than musty books and documents and hours and hours in badly lit archives.

He made her trip sound like some kind of espionage assignment. "At least," her cousin went on, "don't let anyone in Boston know you're a Marsh. It's just too dangerous. If Jonathan Harling finds out—"

"That's the name of the last Harling in Boston?"

Cousin Thackeray nodded somberly. "Jonathan Winthrop Harling."

She grinned. "I look at it this way. What could one little old man who happens to be a Harling do to me?"

J. WINTHROP HARLING climbed the sloping lawn of the gold-domed Massachusetts State House above Boston Common with a sense of purpose. He had come to look at the statue of the infamous Priscilla Marsh. Her tragic death three hundred years ago at the hands of a Harling still colored his family's reputation. It was a part of what being a Harling in Boston was all about.

The wind off the harbor was brisk, even chilly, but he didn't feel it, though he was only wearing the dark gray suit he'd worn to the office.

Although he'd been born and raised in New York and had lived in Boston only a year, he was a stereotypical

Harling in one sense: he made one hell of a lot of money. Sometimes the size of his income, his growing net worth, staggered him. But the Harlings had always been good at making money.

Priscilla Marsh's smooth marble face stared at him in the waning sunlight. She looked very young and very wronged, more innocent, no doubt, than she had been in fact. The sculptor had managed to capture the legendary beauty of her hair, supposedly an unusual shock of pale blond, fine and very straight. She had been hanged on the orders of Cotton Harling when she was just thirty years old.

"Good going, Cotton," Win muttered.

But had she lived and died an ordinary life, Priscilla Marsh would never have inspired an oft-quoted Longfellow poem or a famous 1952 play. Nor would her statue have stood on the lawn of the Massachusetts State House, either.

Win brushed his fingers across the cool stone hair and felt the tragedy of the young Puritan's death. She had been dead less than a day when evidence of her innocence had arrived. Priscilla Marsh hadn't been teaching the young ladies of her neighborhood witchcraft, but how to cure earaches.

Her death should have been a lesson to future Harlings.

A lesson in patience, humility, faith in one's fellow human beings. A warning against arrogance and pride. Against believing in one's own infallibility.

But, Win thought, it hadn't.

HANNAH ARRIVED IN BOSTON without incident and set up housekeeping in a cramped apartment on Beacon Hill. She had traded with a friend, who would get two weeks in Hannah's Maine cottage come summer. The friend, a teacher, was off to Paris with her French class. Things, Hannah decided, were just meant to work out.

Her first stop, bright and early the next morning, was the New England Athenaeum on Beacon Street, across from the Boston Public Garden. It was a private library, supported by just four hundred members and founded in 1892 by, of course, a Harling.

Hannah indicated she was a professional historian and would like to use the library, a renowned repository of New England historical documents.

Preston Fowler, the director, a formal man who appeared to be in his mid-fifties, informed her that the New England Athenaeum was a private institution. Accordingly, she would be permitted into its stacks and rare book room only when she had exhausted all other possibilities and could prove it was the only place that had what she needed. And even then she would be carefully watched.

Hannah resisted the impulse to tell him other private institutions had opened their doors to her in her career. Arguing wouldn't get her anywhere. She needed something that would work. She sighed and said, "But Uncle Jonathan said I wouldn't have any trouble with you."

"Who?" Preston Fowler asked sharply.

"My uncle." She paused more for dramatic effect than to reconsider what she was doing. Then she added, "Jonathan Winthrop Harling."

Fowler cleared his throat, and Hannah was amused at how rigid his spine went. Ahh, the Harling factor. "You—your name is . . . ?"

"Hannah," she said, not feeling even a twinge of guilt. "Hannah Harling."

WIN SETTLED BACK in his soft leather chair and took the call from the elderly uncle whose name he bore. "Hey, there, Uncle Jonathan, what's up?"

Jonathan Harling, who had just turned eighty, got straight to the point. "You going to the New England Athenaeum dinner on Saturday?"

"Wild horses couldn't drag me. Why?"

"Friend of mine says he saw a Harling on the guest list."

"Well, it wasn't me," Win said emphatically. "I haven't even been inside that snooty old place. Your friend must have been mistaken. What about you? You aren't going, are you?"

Uncle Jonathan grunted. "Some of us don't have unlimited budgets, you know."

"I would be happy to buy you a ticket—"

"Damned if I'll accept charity from my own nephew!" the old man bellowed hotly. "Why don't you go, meet a nice woman who'll inspire you to part with some of that booty of yours? How much you worth these days? A million? Two? More?"

Win laughed. "It's more fun to keep you guessing."

Still grumbling, his uncle hung up. Win turned his chair so that he could see the spectacular view of Boston Harbor from his fourteenth-floor window. He watched a few planes take off from Logan Airport across the water. It was a clear, warm, beautiful May afternoon, the kind that made him wonder if he shouldn't call up the New England Athenaeum and get a ticket to its fund-raising dinner, just to see who showed up.

But meeting women was not a problem for him. Contrary to his uncle's belief, Win did not live the life of a monk. No, he had no trouble at all finding women to go out on the town with him, occasionally to share his bed. It was finding the *right* woman. . . .

"Romantic nonsense," he muttered.

BY HER FOURTH DAY in Boston, Hannah had settled into a pleasant routine of research. Preston Fowler himself had invited her to the New England Athenaeum's fund-raising dinner and she'd accepted, despite the rather steep price. But she was supposed to be a Harling and therefore have money. Besides, Fowler himself had begun to help her ferret out information on the Harlings; she had told him she was researching one of her ancestors, Cotton Harling. No point in stirring up trouble by mentioning Priscilla Marsh or the truth about her own identity. She was enjoying the perks of being a Harling.

"Is this your first trip to Boston?" Fowler asked on a cool, rainy morning. He had brought a couple of books to the second-floor table he had reserved for her at a window overlooking the Public Garden.

"Yes," Hannah lied, not without regret. He was being helpful, after all.

"Are you a member of the New York Harlings?"

The New York Harlings? Fowler's eagerness was impossible to miss—the New York Harlings must be rich, she thought—but she had never heard of them. She would have to remember to ask Cousin Thackeray, who still didn't know she was running around Boston claiming to be a Harling. But he had been the one to tell her not to reveal she was a Marsh.

She shook her head. "The Ohio Harlings."

"I see," the New England Athenaeum's director said. He was dressed in a Brooks Brothers suit today, a white on white shirt, wing tip shoes. There was never a hair out of place.

Hannah had invested in a couple of Harling-like outfits in an hour of rushing around on Newbury Street. Now she was afraid to dig out her charge-card receipts to see how much she'd spent. Would the IRS accept them as a business deduction? Preston Fowler would never believe she was a Harling if she kept showing up in her collection of leggings, jeans and vintage T-shirts. Once or twice she might get away with it, but not every day.

As for any real Harlings . . . well, there was only one in Boston, and she wasn't worried about him. Jonathan Winthrop Harling would be old, knobby-kneed and nasal-voiced, with a wardrobe of worn tweeds and holey deck shoes that he would be too cheap to replace. He would have bony hands with a slight tremble, and he'd wear thick glasses with finger smudges on the lenses.

She had him all pictured.

Fowler told her about a painting at the Museum of Fine Arts that she must see, a portrait of Benjamin Harling, the eighteenth-century shipbuilder. Hannah promised to have a look.

Finally he left.

She resumed her scan of a late-nineteenth-century newspaper account of a fistfight between some Harling or other and Andrew Marsh, Cousin Thackeray's grandfather. It involved their divergent opinions about the Longfellow poem on Priscilla Marsh, the Harling insisting it clearly romanticized her, the Marsh insisting it did not. A big mess.

Half paying attention, Hannah suddenly sat up straight. "What's this?"

She went back and reread a blurred, yellowed paragraph toward the end of the article.

In a long-winded way, it said that the Marsh had challenged the Harling to open up "the Harling Collection" to public inspection.

The Harling Collection?

Hannah's researcher's heart jumped in excitement. Now this was news. Something worth checking out. She read further.

Apparently Anne Harling, deceased in 1892, had gathered the family papers from the past three centuries, since the Harlings' arrival in Boston in 1630, into a collection.

What Hannah wouldn't give to get her hands on it!

She carefully copied the information into her notebook and sat looking out at the rain-soaked tulips and budding trees of the Public Garden, wondering what her life had come to that locating a bunch of old documents excited her.

"MR. HARLING?"

Win looked up from his computer and sighed. His young secretary, fresh out of Katherine Gibbs, was clearly determined to shape him into her idea of a suitable executive. He wasn't sure just what his failings were. "You can call me Win, Paula," he said, not for the first time. "What's up?"

"It's the impostor again."

"Where?"

"The Museum of Fine Arts."

"Uncle Jonathan called?"

"While you were in a meeting," Paula confirmed, all business. Win wondered if it had been a good idea to tell her about the unknown Harling who was supposedly attending the New England Athenaeum's fundraising dinner. She had been convinced right from the start that they were dealing with an impostor. "He said to ask you if you had signed up for the lecture series on seventeenth-century American painting that is being offered by the museum. A friend of his knows the instructor and—"

"Yes, I understand. Uncle Jonathan knows everyone." Win tilted back in his chair. "He doesn't think it's a practical joke?"

"No." From her look, neither did Paula. She was tawny-haired and twenty-two and very good at what she did. "It's a woman, Mr. Harling. Trust me."

"Why would a woman pose as a Harling?"

Paula made a face that said what she wanted to do was groan, but groaning didn't fit her code of conduct. "May I speak freely?"

"What is this, a pirate ship? Of course you may."

She took a step closer to his desk, a black modern thing his decorator had picked out. "Mr. Harling, if you don't mind my saying so, I've been with you almost a year now, and it seems to me you don't have much of a clue as to how people around here view your family."

"The Harlings, you mean," he said.

"That's right." She was very serious. "Lots of people, given the chance, would like to take advantage of your wealth and reputation, your position in the financial community. You have breeding—"

"Breeding? Paula, I'm not a horse."

She was too sincere to be embarrassed. "As I said, you don't have a clue."

"Okay, suppose you're right. Suppose someone is trying to take advantage of me. First, why me and not my uncle? Second, why a woman?"

"In answer to your first question," she said, obviously disgusted by his ignorance, "because you are thirty-three and single and your uncle is eighty. Ditto that for the answer to your second question."

"Why can't there be a third Harling in Boston?"

"There isn't."

Win glanced at his computer; his work was beckoning. "So a supposed Harling signed up for a class at the MFA and plans to attend a fund-raising dinner. That doesn't make a conspiracy."

"You wait," Paula said confidently, heading for the door. "There'll be another."

WIN ARRIVED a few minutes late for his weekly lunch with Jonathan Harling at his elderly uncle's private club on Beacon Street, just below the State House. It was a musty, snooty old place with cream-colored walls, Persian carpets, antique furnishings and an aging, largely male clientele. Win would bet he was the youngest one in the place by forty years. The food, however, was passable, if traditional New England fare, and he always enjoyed his uncle's company.

"Sorry I'm late," he said, approaching Uncle Jonathan's table overlooking a stately courtyard. "It's been one of those days. No, don't get up."

Jonathan Harling sank gratefully into his antique Windsor chair. Always a model of integrity and responsibility for his nephew, he was a tall, thin man with eyes as clear at eighty as they had been thirty years ago, when he had been an acclaimed professor of legal history at Harvard. Win knew it had almost killed his uncle when he'd opted for Princeton.

"Name me one day in the past six months that hasn't been 'one of those days,'" the old man grumbled.

Win decided to sidetrack. "It's a busy time of the year. Is the chowder good today?"

Uncle Jonathan already had a bowl in front of him. "It's never good."

"Then why do you keep ordering it?"

"Tradition," he said in a tone that indicated he damned well knew his nephew had no patience with such things.

Win deftly changed the subject. "Any news on our Harling friend?"

"The impostor, you mean. Nothing yet. He's taking his time, making sure he doesn't make a mistake."

"My secretary is convinced it's a she."

Uncle Jonathan mulled that one over. "Good point. I've alerted a number of my friends to keep on the lookout. We don't want him—or her—to start charging fur coats and fast cars to our name. *You* might be able to afford such things, but I can't."

Win let that comment pass. "Have you talked to Preston Fowler at the Athenaeum?"

"Not yet. I just heard about the Museum of Fine Arts incident today. I don't want to start ruffling feathers and end up looking like a fool if it's all just a coincidence."

"But you don't think it is," Win said.

Uncle Jonathan shook his head, serious. "No, I don't."

The waiter came, and Win ordered the roast turkey, his uncle the scrod. Out of the corner of his eye, Win spotted the maître d' leading a lone diner to the table directly behind him.

It was all he could do to remember to tell the waiter to bring coffee.

The lone diner was young and female, so that automatically made her stand out. But in addition she had hair that was long and straight and as pale and fine as corn silk, hair that would make her stand out anywhere. She was slender and not very tall, and she wore a crisp gray suit.

Uncle Jonathan had also noticed her. "Where did she come from?"

"I don't know," Win replied. "I've never seen her before."

"I don't think she's a member. Must be related to a member, though. I wonder who?"

Win shrugged and eased off the subject, having seen the sparkle in his uncle's eye. There was nothing he'd like better than to have his nephew attracted to a woman whose family belonged to the same prestigious private club the Harlings had been members of for all the one hundred fifty years of its existence. Lunch arrived, and Win brought up the Red Sox.

It didn't work.

"Look," Uncle Jonathan said, "she ordered the lobster salad."

The lobster salad was the most expensive item on the limited menu. Win couldn't resist turning in his seat. Her back was to him, maybe three feet away, but he could see her breaking open a steaming popover. Her fingers were long, feminine but not delicate, the nails short and neatly buffed. There was something strangely familiar about her, yet he knew he had never seen her before. He would have remembered.

Their meals arrived, and he turned back to his uncle. "The Red Sox," he said stubbornly, "had a terrible road trip. They're at home this weekend with the Yankees. Are you planning to go?"

"She must not eat lobster very often. She wouldn't stay that thin."

Win sighed. "Of course, the impostor could try to take over our box seats...."

That brought Uncle Jonathan around. "No, I doubt it. He's only left tracks at the Athenaeum and the Museum of Fine Arts. Probably not a baseball fan."

"I don't know, it's possible. I suppose there's not much we can do at this point, except remain on alert. As you say, it's too soon to act." Win tried his turkey; it wasn't very good. "But if there *is* an impostor running around Boston, capitalizing on our name ... well, I'd like to get my hands on him. Or her."

Uncle Jonathan concurred.

By the time the waiter cleared their plates and brought fresh coffee, their conversation was back to the blonde. "Why don't you turn around and introduce yourself? It's not as if you're shy. Invite her over for coffee. Let's find out who she is."

"Uncle Jonathan..."

But he pushed his chair back and grabbed his cane, half getting up. "Miss, excuse me. Our saltshaker's stopped up, and I hate to bother the waiter. Mind if we borrow yours?"

There was nothing Win could do but indulge the old goat. He turned around, and the blonde was there facing him, her eyes huge and green and luminous. She looked a little startled. Who wouldn't? Win took in the high cheekbones and straight nose, the strong chin. Combined, her features made an angular, curiously elegant face. Her skin was pale and clear. Her arresting eyes and hair, however, dominated.

She looked intelligent enough to notice that their table had been cleared. Their waiter was approaching with the coffeepot and Uncle Jonathan's ritual dish of warm Indian pudding, which always looked to Win as if it had come from a cat box.

"Of course," the woman said, and handed over her saltshaker. Win took it.

She turned away.

So much for that.

Win shoved the saltshaker at his uncle. "You're incorrigible."

"Don't you think she looks familiar?"

"Yes," Win said, interested, "I do."

"I can't figure out why. Anyway, she's pretty. Invite her to dinner."

"Uncle..."

"You might never see her again. What if she's the one? You'll have missed your chance."

"If she's 'the one,'" Win said, speaking in a much lower voice than his uncle, who apparently didn't give a damn who heard him, "then there'll be another chance. I believe in fate taking a hand in matters of the heart."

Jonathan snorted. "Romantic nonsense." He waved his spoon. "There, she's leaving. Catch her."

"She's not a trout."

"If she were a tempting stock option you'd never let her get away. Can't you get excited about something that doesn't involve dollar signs?"

Win could. He most definitely could. He was right now. Watching the blonde's hair bounce as she left, the movement of her shapely legs, was not something that lacked consequences. Physical consequences, even. But he didn't share his reaction with his uncle. Instead he said sanely, "I won't come on to a perfect stranger. That could be construed as harassment."

"Only after she tells you to chew dust and you persist. The first time it's just an invitation to dinner."

"On what grounds do I invite her to dinner?"

"Who needs grounds?"

Win groaned. "If she had wanted to meet someone, she wouldn't have come here. This club's known for its elderly membership."

"It's no secret you and I have lunch here on Wednesdays, you know," Uncle Jonathan said thoughtfully. "Maybe she wanted to meet you. That ever occur to you?"

"If she'd wanted to meet me, don't you think she would have said something when you bellowed at her about the salt?"

His uncle was undeterred. "Maybe she would have if you'd said something first."

Win gave up. His uncle was the one indulging in romantic nonsense. The woman had given no indication she was interested in, had recognized or indeed cared if she ever saw either Harling again.

But those eyes. They were unforgettable. And her hair.

What was it about her that was so damned familiar?

Their waiter slipped Win the bill, which he would quietly sign and have put on his account. It was an arrangement they had, in order to keep his uncle from insisting on paying his half, which was just for show. Win knew Uncle Jonathan wouldn't part with a dime if he could get someone else to pay first.

Financially secure though he was, Win found the tab a bit staggering. "Wait just a minute! You've put an extra meal on my bill."

"Well, yes, your . . . Ms. Harling indicated . . ."

Win jumped to his feet. "*Who?*"

"The woman." The waiter nodded to the table just vacated by the silken-haired blonde. "If there's been a mistake . . ."

Uncle Jonathan was reaching for his cane. He was an intelligent man. He plainly knew what was going on. "She's our impostor!"

"Yes," Win said through gritted teeth. He looked at his uncle. "You all right?"

Uncle Jonathan waved him on with his cane. "Go, go. Track down the larcenous little wench."

Win didn't bother arguing with his uncle's choice of words, but simply signed the bill for the entire amount and went.

2

HANNAH WAS BREATHING hard and hoping she was sane again by the time she reached the modern building in the heart of Boston's financial district. Her name was Marsh, she repeated under her breath. Hannah Marsh, Hannah Marsh, Hannah Marsh. She *wasn't* a Harling.

This little visit would straighten everything out. She would go up to Jonathan Winthrop Harling's office, introduce herself, confess if she had to and explain if she could. She had put herself down for the New England Athenaeum's fund-raising dinner to keep Preston Fowler happy, had signed up for the lecture series at the Museum of Fine Arts on the spur of the moment, and realized only after she'd committed herself that she'd better be consistent and go as a Harling.

She didn't know how she'd explain lunch.

The Beacon Street club was one of Jonathan Winthrop Harling's hangouts, and she'd gone there hoping to meet him. Hoping to explain. Hoping to ask him about the Harling Collection. But she didn't even know if he'd been there because she'd frozen up, plain and simple.

That black-eyed rogue behind her had done it. Something about his looks had rattled her. Two hundred years ago he would have run guns for George

Washington. Three hundred years ago Cotton Harling would have had him hanged. He had looked, she thought, decidedly unpuritanical. How could she think, much less confess, with him around?

So she hadn't. And then the waiter had asked if she wanted to put her lunch on the Harling account—she'd had to pretend to be one, of course, to get into the place—and not wanting to blow her cover, she'd said yes.

Now she was a criminal. If the Harlings were all as miserable as Cousin Thackeray had said they were, she could be in big trouble with Jonathan Winthrop.

Then she'd never get a look at the Harling Collection.

The time had come, she told herself as she went through the revolving doors, to come clean, plead for mercy and hope that an eighty-year-old man, even if a Harling, would understand that she was a legitimate, professional biographer. She would make him understand.

She glanced around the elegant wood and marble lobby, then bit her lip when she spotted the armed guards. There were four of them. One behind a half-moon-shaped desk, two mingling with the well-dressed businesspeople flowing in and out of the elevators and revolving doors, another on the mezzanine. He had a machine gun.

An easygoing place, Jonathan Winthrop Harling's office. Hannah had expected a nice old brownstone on Beacon Hill. But probably the old buzzard liked being surrounded by men with guns.

She approached the guard behind the half-moon desk. He was a big, red-faced man, tremendously fit-looking, with curly auburn hair and a disarming spray of freckles across his nose. He didn't look as if he would shoot a woman for pretending to be a Harling, but this was Boston and Hannah just didn't know.

He listened without expression while she explained that she had an appointment with Jonathan Winthrop Harling, but had forgotten which floor he was on.

"Your name?" he asked.

She gulped.

"Ma'am?"

"Hannah," she said. "Jonathan's expecting me."

His eyes narrowed. "Who?"

She'd made a mistake. "Jonathan Winthrop Harling. I'm—I'm Hannah Harling. From Cincinnati. The Midwest Harlings. We..."

She hated lying to men with guns.

The guard picked up the phone. "I'll call Mr. Harling."

"No!"

The old buzzard would swallow his teeth if the guard said one of the Midwest Harlings was here to see him. There were no Midwest Harlings.

"I just need his floor number," Hannah added quickly. "Really."

"And I need to call," the guard said coolly. "Really."

Good, Hannah. Get yourself shot.

She backed away from the desk. "Never mind," she told the guard, manufacturing a smile. "I'll come by another time. Don't bother telling Mr. Harling I was here. I—I'll call him later."

No one followed her through the revolving doors. Her heart was pounding when she reached the plaza in front of the building, but when she looked over her shoulder she didn't see any armed men coming after her.

But she didn't relax.

She wondered what had become of play-by-the-rules Hannah Priscilla Marsh. Cousin Thackeray had warned her about Boston. Maybe she should have listened.

Not wanting to look totally guilty, in case the guard was watching, she lingered at the fountain. It was a warm, beautiful day. Yellow tulips waved in the breeze and twinkled in the sunlight all along the fountain, which sprayed thin arcs of water every few seconds. The effect was calming, mesmerizing.

But she still had half an eye on the revolving doors. A flurry of activity, some shoving, people moving out of the way caught her eye. She turned.

And there he was.

"Oh, no!"

She was off like a shot, adrenaline surging. She didn't know who he was or what he thought she'd done, but she knew instinctively that he was after her, that she couldn't let him catch up with her.

It was her black-eyed rogue from lunch.

He looked fit to be tied. Determined. Dangerous.

Did he work with Jonathan Harling? Were they friends? Did he know she was running around town pretending she was a Harling?

There was no time to think.

She moved fast, pushing her way through a crowd and around the block, vaguely aware that Jonathan Winthrop Harling's building occupied the corner. She came to a side entrance.

She had no choice. None whatsoever. Looking back, she saw her pursuer pounding around the corner, straight for her. She had no idea if he had spotted her, was only aware that this wasn't her city and she didn't know where to hide, didn't want to meet him in a dark, unpopulated alley.

So back into the building she went.

WIN SPOTTED HER going through the revolving doors at the side entrance and moved fast to intercept her.

But when he got back to the lobby, she was gone.

He searched the place with his eyes. The red-haired guard came up to him. "Lose her?"

"She's in here," Win said.

"One of my men must have seen her."

"It's okay." This was his place of business, his space. He couldn't have a green-eyed blonde creating chaos here. "I'll find her myself."

"She doesn't know what floor you're on," the guard informed him. "I wouldn't tell her."

"Thanks."

Where could she have gone? The guard would have seen her if she'd tried to circle back to the front entrance. Win would have seen her if she'd doubled back through the side entrance. The only other options were the ladies' room and the elevators. Surely a guard would have questioned her if she'd tried to get onto an elevator. His was a financial building with moderately tight security.

Hannah Harling of the Midwest Harlings.

The blonde from lunch.

The larcenous little wench, Uncle Jonathan had called her. Win could think of other names.

He posted himself outside the ladies' room just off the lobby and waited.

HANNAH FINISHED booking a trip for two to Vancouver. Her plans, she told the agent, were tentative. The small travel agency off the main lobby was as good a hiding place as any and better than most.

She hated lying, but felt she had little choice.

"When I have everything finalized," the agent, a pleasant woman in her mid-fifties, said, "I should send it up to Jonathan Winthrop Harling. Is that correct?"

"Yes."

"And you're Hannah Harling," she went on.

Hannah didn't respond. She was going to get herself arrested if she wasn't more careful, but avoiding the truth about her real name was certainly preferable to facing the black-eyed man who was after her. He didn't look as if he would listen to any excuses she might have. Had he heard her say she was a Harling at the Beacon Street club? Was he protecting Jonathan Harling?

What if the old man with him at lunch had been Jonathan Harling?

She wished she had never listened to Cousin Thackeray. She wouldn't have been predisposed to say she was a Harling if he hadn't insisted so adamantly that a Marsh was doomed in Boston, "Harling country." But she knew her elderly cousin wasn't responsible. She was responsible for her own actions.

"I hadn't," the agent resumed, "realized Mr. Harling was married."

Married?

To some eighty-year-old man?

Hannah smiled and left without correcting the woman on any of her misconceptions. Surely she would be able to explain Vancouver for two to Jonathan Winthrop Harling. *Yeah, right. Given what you've demonstrated of your character so far, he'll just be delighted to give you access to his family's papers.*

She'd dug one very deep crater for herself.

But what was done was done, and she couldn't hang around in the travel agency forever. Venturing carefully into the corridor, Hannah peered toward the main part of the lobby, where the security guard was posted behind his half-moon desk. She was out of view of the man on the mezzanine with the machine gun. *Thank heaven for small favors.* The other two she couldn't see. They didn't worry her nearly as much as her dark-eyed stranger.

Spotting him, she inhaled sharply.

He was posted at the women's bathroom at the far end of the corridor, not fifty feet from her.

Lordy, she thought, but he was a handsome devil.

Did he think she was hiding in the bathroom? Was he waiting for her? Maybe she was just being paranoid. Either that or she'd outwitted him, she thought, with a welcome surge of victory.

You're not out of here yet, she reminded herself.

She saw him glance at his watch and march toward the bank of elevators, his back to her. She held her breath at the sight of his clipped, angry walk. He did have broad shoulders. And his suit was so well cut it moved with him, made him seem very masculine indeed.... A modern pirate.

Telling herself she was playing it safe, not behaving like a coward, she ducked back into the travel agency to give the elevators time to whisk him back where he belonged.

The travel agent said happily, "I just faxed the information to Mr. Harling's office."

Oh, good, Hannah thought.

She decided to cut her losses for the day and darted out the side entrance before anyone so much as saw her, never mind pinned her to the nearest wall and called the police.

"I WARNED YOU," Paula said, handing Win the fax from the travel agency off the main lobby.

"What is it?" he asked, still too angry to focus on anything other than his frustration at having lost the blonde.

"Reservations for two to Vancouver next month."

"What?"

"You're going to Vancouver for a week. The agency's working out the details of your stay, but from what I can gather, it's going to be very luxurious."

"Paula, I'm not going to Vancouver."

"I know that." She jerked her head in the direction of the offending fax. "But tell Hannah Harling."

Win's eyes focused. He saw two names: Jonathan Winthrop and Hannah Harling. Then the little note from the travel agency downstairs, congratulating him.

On what? For what?

"She's not satisfied with being a long-lost cousin from Cincinnati," his secretary said scathingly. "She wants to be your wife."

THAT EVENING, Hannah opened up a can of soup for dinner, still too stuffed from lunch and too frazzled by her day to want a big meal.

She ate standing up, pacing from one end to the other of her borrowed, Beacon Hill apartment. It wasn't very far. At eye level, three shuttered windows looked onto the brick sidewalk and offered an uninspiring view, nothing like her view of the bay off Marsh Point. The friend who'd lent her the apartment kept a powerful squirt gun on the kitchen windowsill. Hannah had discovered the hard way that it was meant as a handy deterrent to particularly bold dogs, who occasionally did their business without benefit of leash, manners or master.

But the apartment was a quiet, functional place to work, and that, she reminded herself, was her purpose in Boston. Work. Nothing more. She had nothing to hide. She had no bone to pick with the Harlings.

Now she realized she'd blundered badly; she'd let Cousin Thackeray's hyperbole and paranoia get to her. She should never have posed as a Harling.

There was nothing to do but make amends. She had to confess.

First, however, she would lay everything out for her elderly cousin and see what he had to offer by way of advice. Her soup finished, she started for the wall phone in the kitchen.

And stopped, not breathing.

She was sure she recognized the charcoal-covered legs. The deliberate walk. The polished shoes. They were on her sidewalk, directly in front of her middle window.

She moved silently across the linoleum floor and leaned over the sink, balancing herself with one hand on the faucet. She peered up as best she could, trying to get a better look at the passerby as he moved toward the kitchen window.

It was him!

Her hand slipped off the faucet and landed in the sink, wrenching her elbow. Her soup pan, soaking in cold water, went flying. The thud of stainless steel on linoleum was loud enough to be heard at Boston Garden. There was water everywhere.

Hannah swore.

She heard the fancy shoes crunch to a stop on the brick sidewalk. Saw the handsome suit blocking her window. All he had to do was bend down and he'd see her.

She didn't breathe, didn't swear, didn't yell in pain. Didn't make a single, solitary sound.

He moved on.

I'm haunted, she thought, getting ice out of the freezer for her elbow. She threw towels on top of the spilled water and dumped the soup pan back into the sink. How many people in metropolitan Boston? Two million? What were the odds against seeing the same man at lunch, in the financial district, and now, on Beacon Hill at dinnertime?

Hannah waited an hour before going out. She tied a scarf around her head, tucking in every blond hair in case her black-eyed rogue was still out and about and might recognize her. She had to risk it. She needed to walk, to think. She couldn't even concentrate enough to call Cousin Thackeray. What on earth would she tell him? How could she explain her peculiar day, even to him?

Beacon Hill was a neighborhood of subdued elegance, a lovely place to be at dusk, with its steep, narrow streets, brick sidewalks, black, wrought-iron lanterns and Federal Period town houses. Louisa May Alcott had lived here, the Cabots and the Lodges, Boston mayors and Massachusetts senators—and, of course, the Harlings.

Hannah barely noticed the cars crammed into every available parking space, the fashionably dressed pedestrians, but imagined instead the picturesque streets a hundred, two hundred years ago. She knew her ability to give life to the past was the central quality that, critics said, made her biographies not just scholarly, but intensely readable.

Less than a week in Boston, and already her reputation was in jeopardy.

When she came to Louisburg Square, Boston's most prestigious residential address, she turned onto its cobblestone circle. Elegant town houses faced a small private park enclosed within a high wrought-iron fence. Hannah made her way to the house the Harlings had built. It had a bow front and was black-shuttered, its front stoop ending right on the brick sidewalk. Any yard would be in back, one of Beacon Hill's famous hidden gardens.

According to her most recent information, now several years old, the house was owned by a real-estate developer. The Harlings had sold it during the Depression.

Hannah sighed and stared at the softly illuminated interior that was visible through the draped windows. Would the current owner let her have a look at the place? Would she have better luck as Hannah Marsh, biographer, or Hannah Harling of the Midwest Harlings?

She wasn't quite sure why she cared. After all, what did a house built more than a hundred years after Judge Cotton Harling had sentenced Priscilla Marsh to death have to do with her work?

The cream-colored, brass-trimmed front door opened, startling her. She jumped back.

Then felt her heart jump right out of her chest.

Her black-eyed rogue bounded out, wearing nylon running shorts and a black-and-gold Boston Bruins T-shirt.

Never mind getting to blazes out of there, as any sensible woman would have done, Hannah barely managed not to gape at the man's thighs. The muscles were hard and tight, and a thick, sexy scar was carved above the left knee. He looked tough, solid, masculine.

And he recognized her immediately, scarf or no scarf.

"Don't move," he said. "I wouldn't want to have to chase you."

Given that she'd only slipped on a pair of flats and he was wearing expensive running shoes, she doubted she'd get far. And his legs were longer.

She was at a profound disadvantage.

His eyes bored into her. They were black, piercing, intelligent, alive, the kind of eyes that sparked the imagination of a woman more used to examining the lives of dead people. "I won't have you arrested—"

"Good of you," Hannah retorted, just lightly sarcastic.

He was unamused. "You will stop posing as a Harling."

She blinked. "Posing?"

Still no sign of amusement. Whoever he was, he took her little ruse this past week seriously—too seriously for her taste. "Posing," he repeated.

His lean runner's body was taut, and he seemed very sure of himself.

Hannah couldn't let him get the better of her.

"I don't know what you're thinking," she began, doing her best to sound indignant, "but I am a Harling. I'm from Cincinnati. I'm in Boston on a genealogical expedition and—"

He leaned toward her. "Give it up."

"Give what up?"

"You're not a Harling, and if I were you, I'd cut my losses while I still could."

His words grated. "And just who are you to be telling me to do anything?"

He raised his head slightly, looking at her through half-closed eyes.

Something made her swallow and think, for a change.

"You're not . . ." she mumbled, half to herself, "you can't be . . ."

"I'm surprised," he said cockily, "you don't recognize your own husband."

For the first time in her life, Hannah was speechless. A hot river of awareness flowed down her back, burned into every fiber of her.

The black eyes had thrown her off. Cousin Thackeray had said the Harlings were all blue-eyed devils.

But this black-eyed devil said, "Name's Harling."

She swallowed hard, preparing herself for the rest of it.

"J. Winthrop Harling."

He wasn't eighty. He wasn't knobby-kneed. He didn't wear smudged glasses. And he sure as blazes wasn't harmless.

What had she done?

You'll be in Harling country, Cousin Thackeray had warned her. *Just never forget you're a Marsh.*

She pulled off her scarf, letting her hair fall over her shoulders, feeling a small rush of pleasure at the sight of J. Winthrop Harling's widening eyes. But the pleasure didn't last when she realized what she saw in them. Lust. It was the only word for it.

Right now, at that moment, he wanted her.

Cousin Thackeray would croak.

She tossed back her head. "You Harlings will never change. You're the same arrogant bastards you were three hundred years ago. I'm surprised you haven't threatened to have me hanged."

He frowned. "Hanged?"

"It's the Harling way," she quipped, and about-faced. She headed for her street, daring J. Winthrop Harling to follow her.

WIN LET HER GO.

He jogged down to the Charles River and did his three-mile run along the esplanade, his mind preoccupied with the fair-haired, green-eyed impostor. She had as much as admitted that she was no Harling.

Then who was she? A conwoman? A nut? Had one of his friends put her up to this charade as part of some elaborate practical joke?

What was that nonsense about hanging?

Her eyes had seemed even more luminous in the soft lamplight, their irises as green and lively as the spring grass. Half of her had seemed humiliated by having met a real Harling, but the other half had seemed challenged, even angry. She hadn't, he would guess, chosen the Harling name out of admiration.

So what was her game?

Sweating and aching, Win returned to the drafty house he had bought a year ago. It needed work. He could hire the job out, but he wanted to do it himself, with his own hands.

He grimaced, turning on the shower, trying to erase from his mind the image of his hands, not smoothing a piece of wallboard, but the impostor's soft, pale skin . . . touching her lips . . . stroking her throat. . . .

He turned the faucet to cold and climbed in, welcoming the shock of the icy water on his overheated skin. But the heat of his arousal was not easily quenched, and the image remained. Fund-raising dinners, art lectures, his uncle's club, Vancouver, even his own street. The woman had invaded every corner of his life. And now his mind, as well. His body was responding to the simple thought of her tongue intertwined with his.

"She must be a witch," he muttered.

Then he had it.

He no longer felt the cold of the shower. He shut off the water and reached for a towel. He barely noticed the continued swollen state of his arousal.

A witch.

Of course.

The pale, silken hair . . . the green eyes . . . the anger . . . the accusation about threatening to have her hanged . . .

His impostor was a Marsh.

3

HANNAH WAITED until morning, when she'd fully collected her wits, before calling Cousin Thackeray in Maine. "Jonathan Winthrop Harling," she announced to him, "is not the only Harling in Boston."

Her elderly cousin didn't comment right away, and Hannah used the moment of silence to quickly close the shutters, an easy process, since she was on a cordless phone. There was no point in inviting trouble, in case her black-eyed Harling decided to search Beacon Hill for her. She didn't trust him to be above looking into people's windows to find a woman posing as a Harling.

"Well," Cousin Thackeray said carefully, "I could be a bit out of touch. I haven't been to Boston myself in . . . oh, it must be fifty or sixty years."

Hannah gritted her teeth. "Then for all you know Boston could be crawling with Harlings."

"No, no, I doubt that."

"Thackeray," she blurted, "I'm in big trouble."

She told him everything, start to finish. He listened without interruption, except for an occasional gasp or sigh. It wasn't a pretty story.

When she finished, he said, "You've been posing as a *Harling*? Oh, Hannah."

"What's done is done, Thackeray. And now I need to talk to the elder Harling—this Jonathan Winthrop. I still want to examine the Harling Collection."

"Hannah, I want you to listen to me." Her cousin sounded very serious. "The Harling Collection doesn't exist. It never existed. The Harlings made it up to drive folks like you crazy."

"But I have reason to believe—"

"Trust me on this one, Hannah. It doesn't exist."

"If it does, Thackeray, it could well contain information that could provide insight into Cotton Harling's thinking when he signed the order for Priscilla's execution."

Her cousin was apparently unmoved. "It doesn't exist. Give up your search for it at once. Come home, Hannah. If the Harlings find out a Marsh is in town..."

"I'm not finished with my research here," she countered stubbornly.

Cousin Thackeray sighed, clearly not pleased. "You have a plan, I presume?"

"No, not really. I just want to find this old Harling—Jonathan Winthrop—and try to explain everything to him."

"He won't understand."

"Just because he's a Harling?"

"And because you're a Marsh," Thackeray Marsh added.

"Well, I'll have to take my chances with him. I suppose I could have explained to this younger Harling last night...." She inhaled, remembering the black eyes fixed on her, the arrogance. "But it didn't seem the time or place."

Her cousin grunted. "What, was a good hanging tree nearby?"

Hannah made a face. "That's not very funny."

"It wasn't a joke." He sighed. "You'll do what you'll do. You always do. If you need help, give me a holler. You know where I am."

"Thanks." But she could feel her heart thumping, and knew she should heed his advice. "I know I can always count on you."

He muttered something under his breath and hung up. Hannah gathered her materials and stuffed them into her canvas bag, promising herself an ordinary day of research at the New England Athenaeum. No hunting down Harlings today... unless, of course, she got a really good lead on old Jonathan Winthrop, one that would allow her to bypass the black-eyed Harling. She suspected that he was most likely devising his own plan to track *her* down.

AS HE ENTERED the Tiffany reading room of the New England Athenaeum, Win noticed the dour portrait of an ancestor above the mantel. He had to admit there was a family resemblance. Although not a member of the venerable institution, he doubted he would be turned out on his ear.

He introduced himself to the middle-aged woman behind the huge oak front desk. She showed Win back to Preston Fowler's office immediately.

"Mr. Harling," Fowler said, rising quickly from a chair old enough to once have belonged to Ben Franklin, "what a pleasant surprise. What can I do for you?"

"Win, please." He turned on the charm. It was mid-morning, and he had already shocked his secretary by phoning in to say that he'd be late and she should reschedule his morning appointments. "I believe one of my relatives is in town."

"Well, yes, of course. I assumed you knew. I understand she's your cousin...."

"We're not close." His wife in one place, his cousin in another. She should keep her story consistent, Win thought.

"So I've begun to gather. She's been trying to locate your uncle. I haven't given out his private address, of course, but I did tell her she might find him at his club. I hope there's no problem."

"Not at all."

So she was after Uncle Jonathan. No wonder she'd been so shocked when she'd run into him yesterday instead. They were both called Jonathan Winthrop Harling, something Win would guess she hadn't realized.

"She's from Ohio—Cincinnati, I believe."

Like hell. "I see. And she's attending Saturday's fund-raising dinner?"

"Yes, she is. She's not officially a member of the library and wants to repay us for permitting her to use our facilities for her research."

"Her research?"

"She's a historian. I'm not sure precisely what her project is, but she's very interested in the Harling family."

No doubt, Win thought. The more she knew about the Harlings, the better chance she'd have of continuing her ruse of posing as one of them. "Do you have any idea what she wants with my uncle?"

"Just to meet him, I should imagine."

"And she hasn't mentioned me," Win said.

Fowler shook his head. He obviously didn't want any trouble with the Harlings. Win didn't judge the man. He had a tough job, trying to maintain an aging building and a priceless collection on what he could beg from a bunch of tightfisted Boston Brahmins. Uncle Jonathan's idea of a generous donation wouldn't keep the rare book room climate-controlled for a day.

"I'm not sure she's aware you're in Boston," the library director said carefully.

Undoubtedly not. Win spun an old globe, from the days of the British Empire. "Is it too late to purchase a ticket for the fund-raising dinner? I'd like to attend."

Fowler obviously struggled to contain his excitement: it was no secret Win had a hell of a lot more money than his uncle did.

"We would love to have you—I'll attend to the details myself. Oh, and if you would like to meet your cousin, she might be in the stacks. I'm sure I saw her earlier this morning."

Win felt his adrenalin surge, but said nonchalantly, "Really? If you don't mind, I'd like to see her."

"I can send someone after her...."

"No, that's all right. I'll go myself."

HANNAH WAS FLIPPING through a book of fasting sermons from the seventeenth century when she heard footsteps below her. The old-fashioned stacks had been formed by dividing the space between the tall ceilings in two, then making a floor in between of translucent glass and adding curving, wrought iron stairs and bookshelves. It was easy to detect another person wandering about. Only, she thought, this person sounded very purposeful . . . even sneaky.

She closed her book and set it back upon the shelf. She was sitting cross-legged on the thick glass floor, at the far end of a row of shelves. Below her, through the translucent glass, she could see the shadow of a tall figure. It wasn't one of the library staff. She was sure of that.

Listening carefully, not moving, Hannah heard the figure walk steadily up and down the stacks below her. The footsteps never paused, never varied their pace. It was as if whoever was down there was looking, not for a book, but for a person.

Me.

The figure reached the end of the row below her, then she heard the sound of footsteps on metal as it started to climb to her level.

Instinct brought Hannah to her feet. Launched her heart into a fit of rapid beating. Tightened her throat.

The footsteps came closer.

She slipped down to the end of her row and moved soundlessly past the next one, and the next, until she was at the far end, near the stairs.

The figure climbed the last stair and stepped onto her level. It was her black-eyed rogue of a Harling.

Oh, no....

Hannah slipped back behind the shelves and waited, not breathing, while he moved all the way to the end of the stacks. She knew he would then methodically walk up and down each row until he found her.

Then what?

Sweat breaking out on her brow, she heard him start on the far row. She ducked up her row so that he wouldn't spot her when he reached the end of his. She could try to keep this up, but he'd eventually catch up. Why not just pop out and hope she scared him to death? Why not just explain herself? Apologize?

Yeah, and you can get on your knees and beg a Harling for forgiveness while you're at it.

Priscilla Marsh hadn't begged. She'd gone to her death with her pride and dignity intact.

Hannah decided to take what little pride and dignity she had left and get the blazes out of here. He'd hear her on the stairs—no question about it. But she'd have a head start, she knew her way around the library, and if she was lucky...

Since when can a Marsh count on luck around a Harling?

She had to count on her wits . . . and maybe on a little gall.

Speed being more critical than silence, she darted down the row and hit the stairs at a full gallop, taking them two and three at a time.

Above her, she heard her pursuer curse.

She swung down to the next level and scooted through the stacks, zigzagging her way to the small corridor in the far right corner. Preston Fowler had loaned her the key to the rare book room. She came to the heavy door that marked its entrance, stuck in the key, and, relying on stealth, quietly pulled the door open and slipped inside.

Without turning on the light, she pressed her ear against the door and waited.

WIN FIGURED she'd locked herself in the rare book room. He also figured his uncle would never forgive him if he made a scene in the venerable New England Athenaeum by hauling a pretty, blond-haired Marsh out by her ear. Preston Fowler would have questions that Win couldn't answer and Hannah Marsh, if that was her name, no doubt wouldn't answer.

So he rapped on the door and said, "I know you're in there."

Naturally she didn't answer.

"You haven't stopped pretending you're a Harling," he went on. "Until you do, I have no intention of leaving you alone."

He waited, just in case she had something to say.

Apparently she didn't.

"By the way, I would say you have my uncle and me confused. We're both named Jonathan Winthrop Harling."

He heard a muffled thud. Had Ms. Hannah pounded her head against the door? He would guess he knew more about her and her devious plans than she expected him to know. Certainly more than she wanted him to know.

"You'd better leave my uncle out of this," he said in his deadliest voice. "I won't warn you again on that score."

Her voice came to him through the door, sounding very clear and surprisingly close: "What're you doing? Tying the noose even now?"

The woman was incorrigible.

In no mood to make her life any easier, Win tiptoed away, so she wouldn't know he had gone.

HANNAH SWEATED IT OUT in the rare book room for another hour.

There were two Jonathan Winthrop Harlings in Boston. All her leads had pointed her in the direction of the wrong one, and as far as she could tell, she was doomed.

Doomed.

But when she went back down to the main reading room, no one treated her like an impostor. Preston Fowler and his staff apparently continued to believe she was a Harling, which was a relief, if a small one. It meant, she knew, that the younger Jonathan Winthrop Harling planned to deal with her himself, in his own good time.

Hannah had no intention of waiting like the proverbial lamb for the slaughter.

On her way out, Preston Fowler said, "We'll see you tomorrow night at the dinner, Ms. Harling."

She smiled. "I'm looking forward to it."

She realized she would need a dress. Her Harling clothes were all for day, and her Hannah Marsh clothes—*my clothes,* she reminded herself—were too casual. So she headed off to Newbury Street, just a few blocks down from the New England Athenaeum. It was one of Boston's most chic and high-priced shopping districts. There wouldn't be much she could afford.

Her black-eyed Jonathan Winthrop Harling, however, could probably buy out the whole street and have plenty left over.

WIN HAD A HELL OF A TIME trying to concentrate that afternoon, and it was almost with relief that he greeted a grim-faced Paula bringing him news of another bit of larceny performed by Hannah of the Midwest Harlings.

"Is she my cousin today," he asked, "or my wife?"

His secretary didn't seem to appreciate his wry humor. "Your wife. The owner of the shop on Newbury Street where you buy your ties just called. A woman fitting the description of the impostor was in earlier and bought a black evening dress on your tab. He faxed me the bill." Paula handed it over. "You will note that she signed her name as Mrs. Hannah Harling."

"Arnie didn't believe her?"

"Oh, no, he believed her. He just called to congratulate you on your wedding. I think he's hurt he wasn't invited."

Win looked at the bill and inhaled, controlling an urge to pound his desk or throw things. The price of the dress was staggering. It was, he knew, Hannah Marsh's way of thumbing her nose at him.

"I was the one who had him fax the bill," Paula said.

"Did you give him a reason?"

She shook her tawny curls. "He should have asked for identification or at least called you before he let her have the dress. She must be awfully convincing."

For sure. Arnie was no pushover. Still, he wasn't alone in not wanting to annoy a Harling. "Call Arnie back," Win instructed her. "Tell him Hannah jumped the gun and we're not married yet."

Paula's eyes widened. "Yet?"

"The point is, I will pay for the dress. This impostor isn't Arnie's problem. She's mine."

THE DRESS WAS AWFUL, and Hannah decided she couldn't wear it. It was too . . . Boston. Too matronly. Too something. She stood in front of the full-length mirror in her borrowed bedroom an hour before the New England Athenaeum dinner and tried to figure out what wasn't right about a dress that had cost as much as this one.

She had bought it in a fit of pique, when she'd only wanted to strike out at Jonathan Winthrop Harling. Now the Harlings really had grounds for throwing her in jail. But better to hang for a thousand-dollar dress, she'd decided, than a twenty-dollar lunch.

Was she crazy?

Not only was the dress not her style, it also wasn't, in fact, hers. Never mind that it was in her possession.

Harling money had—or would—pay for it. She hadn't even removed the tags.

And wouldn't. She would take the thing back on Monday. Twenty-four hours of sitting alone in her borrowed apartment, doing her work, being the studious, law-abiding biographer she was, had enabled her to think. Not even a Harling would turn her into an out-and-out thief.

A smarter decision would have been not to go tonight. The prospect, however remote, of bumping into her black-eyed Harling on his own territory didn't thrill her. But how could she just drop everything and head back to Maine? It just wasn't in her to run.

She rummaged around in her closet and found the dress she'd picked up at a vintage clothing store in Harvard Square. It was not a Harling dress, and it hadn't cost a thousand dollars. It hadn't even cost twenty.

But it was her.

"YOU'RE SURE she's a Marsh?" Uncle Jonathan asked when Win picked him up. Naturally his uncle had insisted on going to the Athenaeum's fund-raising dinner, once he knew their impostor was potentially a Marsh and would be there.

Win nodded grimly. "I'm positive."

"I should have guessed it myself. The blond hair's a dead giveaway."

"You can hardly suspect every blonde you see of being a Marsh without further evidence."

"You'd better watch yourself, Winthrop." Uncle Jonathan climbed into the front passenger seat. "If she's a Marsh, she's after something. Any idea what?"

"None."

"The Marshes have never let us forget Priscilla. They refuse to understand that Cotton was a man of his times, a flawed human being just doing his job."

Win frowned at his uncle. "He had an innocent woman hanged."

"He wasn't the first, nor the last."

There was no point in arguing. Win pulled into traffic, trying to concentrate on the road and not on what was coming up this evening.

"Think she'll risk showing up tonight?" his uncle asked.

Win had already considered the question, given what had transpired yesterday morning, but it had only one answer. "She wouldn't miss it."

HANNAH ARRIVED EARLY at the exclusive seafood restaurant on the waterfront where the New England Athenaeum's fund-raising dinner was being held. Preston Fowler greeted her warmly. Before he could introduce her to anyone as a Harling, she slipped off to the bar, ordered a glass of white wine and found her table. Mercifully, it was at the far end of the room, but still had a good view of the entrance.

She sipped her wine, watching Boston's upper crust filing in, dressed in its spring finery. She saw a dress much like the one she had rejected. It looked curiously right on its owner, just as it had looked wrong on her.

What a long night she had ahead of her, she thought, if all she had to do was notice what people were wearing. . . .

An old man with a cane shook hands with Preston Fowler. Hannah shifted in her chair, her interest piqued. She had seen him somewhere before.

Salt, she thought, for no apparent reason.

Lunch at the private club on Beacon Street.

Her heartbeat quickened, her fingers stiffened on her wineglass, and she said to herself, "The old man with—"

But she didn't finish.

Across the room, the younger Jonathan Winthrop Harling's black eyes nailed her to her seat.

"Oh, no," Hannah whispered.

Her first impulse was to tear her eyes away and pretend she hadn't seen him, but she resisted just in time and met his gaze head-on. She even smiled. She made everything about her say he didn't intimidate her. She could take on him—a Harling—and win.

If ever a pair of eyes could burn holes in someone, it would be the two fixed on her. Hannah felt an unwelcome, unbidden, primitive heat boiling up inside her. There was something elemental at stake here, she thought, something that had nothing to do with Harlings or Marshes or three-hundred-year-old grudges.

She raised her wineglass in a mock greeting, then took a slow, deliberate sip.

He was past Preston Fowler in a flash, threading his way through the crowd, aiming straight for her. His steps were long and determined, as if he'd just caught someone picking his pocket.

Then he was upon her.

The man, Hannah thought, strangely calm, was breathtaking. His dark suit was understated, sophisticated, highlighting the blackness of his hair and eyes, making him look all the richer and more powerful. To be sure, he was a descendant of robber barons and rogues, but also of an infamous seventeenth-century judge who'd hanged one of her own ancestors.

"I like the daffodils," he said in a low, dark voice.

"Do you?" She fingered the two she'd tucked into her hair; it was an un-Brahminlike touch that went with her cream-colored, twenties tea dress. "I thought they were fun."

"They didn't go with your Newbury Street dress?"

So he knew already. She licked her lips. "Not really, no."

"You're a thief," he said simply, "and a conwoman."

She tilted her head to a deliberately cocky angle. "You know so much about me, do you?"

His eyes darkened, if that was possible. "I should, shouldn't I? We're supposed to be married."

Her mouth went dry. "I never said . . ."

"You didn't have to, did you? People assumed." He moved closer, so that she could see the soft black leather of his belt. "I wonder why."

The old man with the cane stumbled up to them, saving Hannah from having to produce a credible response when she could still barely speak. "So you're our Cincinnati Harling," he said.

She managed a smile. "Word travels fast."

"This is my uncle," his nephew said, his tone daring her to persist. "Jonathan Harling."

She put out a hand to the old man. "I'm Hannah. It's a pleasure."

"Delighted to meet you. Welcome to Boston." He surprised her by placing a dry kiss upon her cheek, his eyes—Harling blue—gleaming with interest, missing nothing. He turned to his nephew. "You two have met?"

"Not formally," Hannah replied.

"No?" The old man clapped a hand on the younger Harling's shoulder. "This is my nephew, Win. J. Winthrop Harling."

So it was true. There *were* two Jonathan Winthrop Harlings in Boston. Oh, what a mistake she'd made.

"It's a pleasure," she said, refusing to let the situation get the better of her.

But Win Harling murmured, "The pleasure's mine," and bent forward, kissing her low on the cheek. To all appearances, no doubt, it was a perfunctory kiss, not unlike his uncle's. Hannah, however, felt the warm brush of his tongue on the corner of her mouth, his hard grip as he took her hand. And she felt her own response; it was impossible to ignore. Her mind and body united in a searing rebellion, imagining, feeling, that warm brushing, not discreetly, against the corner of her mouth, but openly, hotly, against her tongue, against other parts of her body.

"If Priscilla Marsh was anything like you, Hannah Marsh," Win Harling said in a rough, low voice, "I can see what drove Cotton Harling to sign her hanging order."

4

THE WOMAN WAS QUICK. Win would give her that much. She gave him a haughty look and threw back her shoulders regally, or as regally as anyone could manage in a silk tea dress from the twenties. The daffodils in her hair didn't help matters. But she said, "I don't know what you're talking about."

He laughed. He couldn't help himself.

She thrust her chin at him. He could still see the flush of pink, high on her cheeks, from his kiss. Obviously it had as powerful an effect on her as it had on him. "Why did you call me Hannah—who?"

He decided to indulge her. "Marsh."

"And Priscilla—it was Priscilla, wasn't it?"

"Yes."

"This Priscilla Marsh. Who is she?"

"Your great-great-great-great—oh, I don't know, I'd give it five greats—grandmother. She was hanged by a Harling three hundred years ago."

"I see," she said, apparently trying her damnedest to sound confused. Win knew she wasn't confused at all.

"Her statue is on the State House lawn."

"Oh!" Hannah smiled suddenly, as if finally getting it. "You mean the witch."

Look who was calling who a witch, Win thought, but kept his mouth shut. He was already out over two thousand dollars, thanks to Priscilla's great-whatever and was beginning to feel the bewitching effects of her eyes, her luscious, pink mouth.

"I've read about her," Hannah said.

"Every real Harling knows about Priscilla Marsh and Judge Cotton Harling."

"I don't."

"You're not a real Harling. You're a Marsh."

She sighed. "Well, I'm not going to argue with you. Shouldn't you and your uncle be finding your seats?"

Uncle Jonathan had busied himself tracking down a couple of drinks. Win sat down in the empty chair next to Hannah Marsh. "Preston Fowler thought the Harlings should sit together."

"How nice," she said, clearly not meaning it. She pursed her lips, trying to buy time, Win suspected, to think of a way to wriggle out of the tight spot she'd squeezed herself into. "If you're so certain of who I am, why haven't you told anyone?"

"You're a smart woman. Figure that one out for yourself."

"With a Harling, it usually boils down to reputation."

Win indicated his uncle, who was making his way through the crowd, carrying two drinks. "If it weren't for him, I'd stand right up on this table and expose you to everyone here for the lying thief you are. But Uncle Jonathan . . ." He narrowed his eyes on her and saw the spots of pink in her cheeks deepen under his penetrating gaze. "He deserves better."

"I can explain, you know. Or won't you give me the chance?"

"What mitigating circumstances might there be for you to charge an expensive dress to my account?"

Her lips parted slightly, her eyes shone. She dragged her lower lip under her top teeth, a habit, Win guessed, when she was caught red-handed. "You asked for it," she challenged him. "There isn't a court in the country that would convict me—unless a Harling was the presiding judge."

"You have to be a Marsh. Only a Marsh would hold someone responsible for what one of their ancestors did three hundred years ago."

She shrugged, neither accepting nor denying his accusation.

Uncle Jonathan arrived with the drinks. "Here you go, Winthrop. Did I miss any excitement?"

"No, not at all." His eyes didn't leave Hannah. "We were just discussing genealogy."

"Boring stuff." Uncle Jonathan sniffed. "Let the dead bury the dead, I say."

Since when? No one was more adamant on the subject of the Marshes' long-standing grudge against the Harlings than Win's uncle. Win glanced at him but said nothing.

"Well, Miss Harling," his elderly uncle said, "how do you like our fair city so far?"

She graced him with one of her beguiling smiles. Her eyes skimmed over Win, as if he were a cockroach she was pretending she hadn't noticed. "Please," she said, "just call me Hannah."

"My pleasure."

Win scowled at his uncle; he knew the woman was a liar and very likely a Marsh, yet he was still trying to charm her. She might look innocent, and she certainly was attractive, but Win wasn't fooled. She'd already cost him too much time and money.

Hannah gestured toward the glittering view of Boston Harbor. "Boston's a lovely city. I'm glad I can appreciate other places without wanting to give up my own life. I know people too afraid to appreciate somewhere else, because they believe it might make them think less of where they live, and others who can only appreciate places they don't live."

Uncle Jonathan stared at Hannah for a few seconds, blinked, sipped his drink and looked at Win, who from years of experience with his uncle already knew what was coming. "What did she say?"

"She likes Boston but doesn't want to live here," he translated, turning to Hannah. "Uncle Jonathan's a bit hard of hearing."

"I'm not. I just didn't understand what in hell she was saying."

Win wondered if he'd be as blunt in his eighties or have as tolerant a nephew. What Hannah was doing, he knew, was saying whatever popped into her head to keep the conversation going before one of the real Harlings at the table decided to call her bluff in public.

"I'm sorry," she apologized quickly, "I've had a long day."

"You're not going to plead a stomachache and make a fast exit, are you?" Win challenged her with an amused grin.

Her luminous eyes fastened on him, any hint of embarrassment gone from her cheeks. There was only anger. The zest for a good fight. "You'd like that, wouldn't you?"

"Just wondering how hot it will have to get before you bow out."

"I don't care what you think. I know who I am."

"And who is that?"

She gave him a small, cool, mysterious smile. "That's for me to know and for you to find out."

Before Win could respond, Preston Fowler came up between them and clapped a hand upon each of their shoulders. "You found each other all right, I see. Glad you could make it. People are delighted to have the Harling family active in the New England Athenaeum again. Hannah, have you talked to your cousin and uncle about your family history? Jonathan here is quite an authority. He might have family papers pertinent to your research that aren't part of our collection."

He spotted another couple entering late and made his apologies, quickly crossing the restaurant.

Uncle Jonathan looked at Hannah. "Didn't know I had a niece in Cincinnati."

Win watched her smooth throat as she swallowed. She said, "I sort of exaggerated our relationship, so I could use the library for my research."

"Sort of?" Win asked wryly.

She scowled at him. "Believe what you want to believe."

"I will."

"What kind of research?" Uncle Jonathan asked.

"Oh, I'm just looking into my roots."

"Why?"

"Curiosity."

Uncle Jonathan sniffed. He pulled at Win's sleeve and whispered, "She's a Marsh, all right. I know just what she's after."

Hannah was frowning, obviously certain Jonathan Harling wasn't saying anything positive. Win, seated between them, turned to his uncle. "What's that?"

"The Harling Collection."

Win had never heard of it.

"I'll explain later," Uncle Jonathan told him, just as Hannah Marsh saw her opening and jumped to her feet.

Win grabbed her by the wrist with lightning speed. "Don't leave," he urged amiably. "You paid for dinner with your own money."

She licked her lips guiltily.

Win gritted his teeth.

"I started to pay with my own money," she explained, "but then I . . . well, one of the staff asked me if they should just send the bill along to you, and I said sure, why not?"

He didn't release her wrist. He didn't know how she managed to look so damned innocent. So justified.

"I also put you down for a hundred-dollar donation," she added.

"Sit."

"You won't make a scene. I know you won't."

"Sit down, *now*."

She batted her eyelids at him, deliberately, cockily. "Shall I beg, too?"

"It could come to that."

He spoke in a low, husky voice, and it was apparently enough to drop Hannah Marsh back into her chair. The spots of pink reappeared in her cheeks. Her breathing grew rapid, light, shallow. She drew her lower lip once more under her top teeth.

"I'm going to find out what you're after," Win said. "And if I have to, I'll stop you."

She gave him a scathing look. "Spoken like a true Harling."

It wasn't a compliment.

HANNAH GOT OUT her checkbook the moment she returned to her Beacon Hill apartment and wrote out a check to J. Winthrop Harling for every nickel she owed him.

When she had refused their offer of a ride home, Win Harling and his uncle had insisted on getting her a cab. She was quite sure they'd heard her give her address and wished, belatedly, she'd lied. But she was getting tired of lying.

She was not a liar. She was not a thief.

She had merely adopted an unwise strategy, that was all. Pretending to be a Harling had been a tactic. An expedient. She wasn't out to get the Harlings. She just wanted to write the definitive biography of Priscilla

Marsh. She, Hannah Marsh, had always played by the rules. She didn't look for trouble.

But she'd found it in spades, hadn't she?

Her check made out, her bank account drawn down to next to nothing, she called Cousin Thackeray in southern Maine. She was still wearing her twenties tea dress.

Thackeray answered on the first ring.

"I'm in trouble," she began, then told him everything.

Her cousin didn't hesitate to offer his advice when she finished. "Come home."

It was tempting. She could picture him in his frayed easy chair, with rocky, beautiful Marsh Point stretched before him. From her own cottage nearby, she could see the rocky shoreline, tall evergreens, wild blueberry bushes, loons and cormorants and seals hunting for food. Even now she could conjure up the smell of the fog, taste the salt in it. Marsh Point was the closest thing she had ever had to a real, permanent home. She would go back. There was no question of that.

But not yet.

"I can't," she said before she could change her mind. "I have a job to do and I'm going to do it. I won't be driven from Boston by anyone."

"Driven?" There was a sharpness, a sudden protectiveness, in Thackeray's voice that made her feel at once wanted and needed, a part of the old man's life. He was family. "Have the Harlings threatened you?"

"Not in so many—well, yeah, in so many words. But don't worry. I can handle myself."

"Shall I drive down?"

Just what she needed. An eighty-year-old man who hated cities, particularly hated Boston, and really and truly hated the Harlings. He would, at the very least, get in the way. And she doubted he could do anything to get her out of hot water with Win Harling.

"No, I'll be fine."

He hissed in disgust. "You're not still after that Harling Collection, are you?"

She sighed. "I'd like to know at least if it exists."

"Can't you take my word for it that it doesn't?"

"Cousin Thackeray..."

"Come home, Hannah. You've done enough research on Priscilla. Just pack up and come home."

Although he was over a hundred miles away, and couldn't see her, Hannah shook her head. "You yourself have said that for the past three hundred years the Harlings have been tough on Marshes who don't kowtow to their power and money. Well, I won't. I'll leave Boston when I'm ready to leave Boston and not a minute sooner."

Cousin Thackeray muttered something about her stubborn nature and hung up.

Hannah was too wired to sleep. Work, she knew, was always the best antidote for a distracted mind. But when she sat at her laptop computer, she thought not of Priscilla Marsh and Cotton Harling, but of J. Winthrop Harling. His searing black eyes. His strong thighs. His sexy, challenging smirk.

Such thinking was unprofessional and unproductive.

Definitely not scholarly.

And as for objectivity... How could she be objective about a man who made her throat go tight and dry, even when she just looked at him? Win Harling could have passed for a rebel who'd helped rout the British, dumped tea into Boston Harbor, tarred and feathered Tories. He was tough and sexy and didn't fit her image of a Harling at all.

Clearly she needed to restore her balance and perspective. But how?

"Give the bastard his money," she muttered, "and hope it makes him happy."

"IT'S A SHAME," Uncle Jonathan said, having agreed to meet his nephew for Sunday morning breakfast, "that an attractive woman like that—bright, gutsy, clever—turns out to be a Marsh."

Win blew on his piping-hot coffee, then took a sip. The café at the bottom of Beacon Hill wasn't crowded, but he had still chosen a table at the back, in case Ms. Hannah, apparently also a Beacon Hill resident, blundered in. He needed to concentrate; he'd found he couldn't when she was near.

"If she wasn't a Marsh," his uncle continued, "she just might be the woman for you, Winthrop. She'd make you think about something besides work, I'd allow."

She already had, but Win said, "Uncle Jonathan, I didn't ask you here to discuss my love life. Now..."

"You need a woman."

Win sighed. "That's a rather blunt statement."

"It's true. You're waiting for fate to take a hand and present you with the woman of your dreams. I say she's out there somewhere and you need to hunt her down."

"Like a buffalo?"

"More like an antelope, I think. Maybe a tigress."

"Uncle Jonathan . . ."

"Well, Win, what can I say? You work too hard. You don't pay enough attention to your personal life. Dating women isn't the same as finding the woman meant for you. And don't tell me that's romantic nonsense, because it's not."

Win knew a change of subject was in order. He didn't want to argue, and not just because he didn't want to sit through another of his uncle's lectures on marriage and little ones. Anything Win said would bring up, however indirectly, Uncle Jonathan's own unhappy life. He had lost his wife to cancer twenty-five years ago, his only child, a daughter—a cousin Win had adored—to a car accident ten years back. The kind of life Jonathan wanted for his nephew meant that Win would have to set himself up for tragedy. Right now he preferred to keep his risks financial.

"Tell me about the Marshes," he said.

That distracted his uncle. He poured cream into his coffee and began a lecture on the Marsh-Harling feud of the past three hundred years, sounding like the history professor he'd once been. Win listened carefully.

"I wouldn't think," he said after a while, "that reasonable people would blame an entire family for the conduct of one of its ancestors. Right or wrong, Cotton's been dead a long time."

"The Marshes will capitalize on his mistake whenever they see an opening. That's how they ended up with a chunk of prime southern Maine real estate that's rightly ours."

"Ours? What do you mean?"

"About a hundred years ago the Marshes swiped a lovely piece of coastal land from the Harlings. They stole the deed from us and claimed they'd bought the land first. No one could prove otherwise. It's theirs to this day." He grimaced. "They call it Marsh Point."

"And the Harling Collection," Win said. "Tell me about it."

"About the same time the Marshes appropriated our land in Maine, a Harling—Anne Harling—gathered the family papers together into a collection."

"I never knew—"

Uncle Jonathan held up a hand, stopping him. "It's never been proven to exist. It disappeared not long after Anne finished putting it together. Nobody's ever produced a credible theory of what happened to it."

"And you think our Hannah Marsh is after it?"

"Yep."

Win shook his head. "It doesn't explain her behavior. Why would she lie to us and steal from us if she expected us to hand over the Harling Collection for her to examine?"

His uncle lifted his bony shoulders, then let them drop; he sighed heavily. "She doesn't expect us to hand it over."

"What do you mean?"

"I mean," his uncle announced, "she plans to *steal* it."

HANNAH ENDURED a disturbingly quiet Sunday. Twice she ventured into Louisburg Square. Nothing seemed out of the ordinary. But then, how would she know? The Harling House stood bathed in spring sunshine, giving away none of its secrets. She debated venturing up the steps and sticking her check into its mail slot. It would mean a lean winter ahead, but would restore her sense of pride. But she decided against leaving it. It had her name imprinted at the top, and she wasn't sure she wanted Win Harling to have her name confirmed for him, at least, not yet. First she had to find a way of explaining what she'd done, making him—or his uncle—understand her motives.

By Monday morning she'd decided Win Harling couldn't learn much more about her than he already suspected. But she remained on her guard. She couldn't relax. If anything, the fund-raising dinner on Saturday could only have stimulated his desire to best her.

Stimulated his desire?

She cleared her throat, reacting to the unfortunate choice of words, and tried to dismiss the possibilities, but dozens of images flooded her mind.

Work. She had to keep working.

But when she arrived at the Athenaeum for a morning of what she'd promised herself would be disciplined research, a message was waiting for her. It was a note scrawled in black marker on a scrap of computer paper.

I suggest you come by my office in the financial district today at noon. We need to discuss the

Harling Collection and Marsh Point. If you value
your reputation, you won't be late. I know who
you are.

It was signed, arrogantly, just with Win Harling's
initials, JWH.

Hannah stood rock still, feeling every drop of blood
drain out of her. She read the note twice.

First of all, she now knew why he'd been in the well-
armed building in the financial district the other day;
his office, not his uncle's, was there. Probably his uncle was retired and no longer had an office. Hannah
hated making a mistake in her research, but never had
one been as costly as this one.

"Well, no use crying over spilt milk," she muttered,
reflecting that a lot more than milk could be spilled by
the end of this affair.

Second, the Harling Collection. He'd figured out she
was after it. Well, that she could understand. She had
made no bones about looking into the Harling family
history, and so could be expected to want to examine
the Harling Collection, if it existed. Still, she would
have preferred to have a chance to explain her real reasons for wanting access to it before Win Harling found
her out. But so be it.

The mention of Marsh Point, however, she didn't
understand. Why would he want to discuss Marsh
Point? Did he know that was where she lived?

And just who did he think she was?

The library assistant who had handed her the note
said, "He also left a book for you."

It was a copy of her biography of Martha Washington.

The bastard knew.

He knew!

"Well," Hannah muttered under her breath, "it's not as if you didn't see it coming."

But to threaten her reputation . . .

How like a Harling.

"Is something wrong, Ms. Harling?" Preston Fowler asked, emerging from his office.

"No. Not at all." She crumpled the note, stuffing it into the pocket of her squall jacket, and turned the book so that Fowler couldn't see the name of its author. She forced a smile. "Thanks for asking."

"Did you enjoy the dinner Saturday?"

"Yes—yes, I did. The food was wonderful, and I enjoyed having the chance to be with my relatives." She smiled, hoping she didn't look as flustered as she felt, but knew she'd always been particularly good at thinking on her feet. A Marsh trait, according to Cousin Thackeray. Of course, if she had listened to him, she might not be in the crummy position she was in right now. She'd be home in Maine, where she belonged. "If you'll excuse me, I'd like to get to work."

"Of course. Let me know if I can be of any assistance."

Would he be so willing to help if he knew she was Hannah Marsh and not Hannah Harling?

But she had a couple of hours before noon and refused to fall victim to obsessions about J. Winthrop Harling. Instead she tucked her notebook under her arm and proceeded to the second floor to the rare book room; the small, secure, climate-controlled space where Win Harling had trapped her the other day.

Amid her musty books, she began to relax. Come what might in her life, she always had her work.

She had already examined the most pertinent documents stored in the room, but there were several peripheral books and documents she wanted to look at. She got started.

After a relatively peaceful hour, disturbed only by moments of having to stomp on her unruly thoughts, she located a history of colonial Boston written in the early nineteenth century. On the inside front cover she spotted, in a faded handwriting, the name Jonathan Winthrop Harling and an address in the Back Bay section of Boston, just around the corner from where she was right now.

Win's uncle Jonathan. The old man with the cane. The man Hannah had intended to find in the first place, the only Harling supposed to be still in Boston. He must have donated the volume.

He had seemed reasonably charming on Saturday evening, and was still her best lead to the Harling Collection. If he hadn't moved, she could look him up herself, instead of going through his black-eyed, suspicious nephew. He might listen to her explanation of her behavior during the past week, to her legitimate reasons for wanting to examine the Harling Collection. He wouldn't threaten her reputation.

Neither would he threaten her peace of mind, create the kind of mental and physical turmoil his nephew did.

He wasn't young and good-looking and too damned sexy for *her* own good.

She had time, if she hurried, to try and see Jonathan Harling before her summons to the Boston financial district and the offices of J. Winthrop Harling. She gathered her papers, stuffed them into her satchel and headed out, hardly stopping to say goodbye to Preston Fowler.

Built on fill from the top of Beacon Hill, the Back Bay consisted of a dozen or so streets beyond the Public Garden, within easy walking distance. Jonathan Harling lived in a stately Victorian brownstone on the sunny side of Marlborough Street. Once a single-family dwelling, the building had been broken up into apartments, probably shortly before or during World War II. The name HARLING was printed next to a white doorbell, which Hannah rang.

There was no answer.

Her spirits sagged. Just her luck. She had hoped she could explain her situation and get him to contact his nephew to have him call off his witch-hunt. If she were particularly persuasive, she might get the old man to talk to her about the Harling Collection and forgive her for her many transgressions. She *would* pay back his nephew.

She considered waiting on his front stoop until he returned, then realized that if she did, she would never make the financial district by noon. Win Harling would only hunt her down. She owed it not to him but to herself to find out what he knew about her, how he'd

learned it, whom he'd told and—most important—
what he'd meant by his reference to Marsh Point.

Uncle Jonathan would have to keep.

5

By THE TIME she reached the modern federal building and its armed guard, an appropriately blustery wind was blowing off the water and dark clouds had rolled in. Springtime in New England. Hannah hunched her shoulders against the cold. She had on a lightweight black squall jacket, black gabardine pants and a pale yellow silk shirt, a little less the proper Bostonian than on her previous visit to the financial district, but still not quite herself. Cousin Thackeray, she remembered, had insisted the Harlings and their crowd were a bunch of tightwads who considered new clothes tackily nouveau riche. Dowdy, worn-out, once-expensive clothes were the mark of a true Boston Brahmin. They'd accept her a lot quicker, he'd maintained, if she could show off a few moth holes. Hannah had refused his offer to beat her clothes on the rocks to make them look more authentically "old money."

Cousin Thackeray...

She couldn't have her feud with Win Harling touch him.

The red-haired guard grinned at her, not making a move for his gun as he might have been expected to, given their last meeting. "Go right on up. Fourteenth floor."

Hannah gave him an I-told-you-so smirk, but there was nothing in his expression that indicated he thought she had the upper hand. She dashed for the elevator and blamed its fast ascent to the fourteenth floor for the slightly sick feeling in her stomach and her sudden lightheadedness. *Win knows about the Harling Collection...about Marsh Point....*

What could he have found out about Marsh Point?

Had Cousin Thackeray neglected to tell her something that he should have?

Checking the floor directory, she found her way to Win's office suite, entering a large, airy, L-shaped room, arranged so that both the reception area and corner office had windows with views of the city and the fountain plaza below.

A young woman greeted Hannah, who was a good ten minutes late. "Mr. Harling's waiting."

Hannah sensed the secretary's disapproval; she obviously didn't like anyone keeping Mr. Harling waiting. The younger woman led the way, pushing open his door in an exaggeratedly professional manner she'd either learned in secretarial school or had seen in old Joan Crawford movies.

J. Winthrop Harling's office was spacious, modern and spare, and Hannah was struck by its contrast to her own rustic, cluttered space overlooking Marsh Point. It was just more evidence that the two of them led totally different lives, and that she was an intruder. She was on his turf, and she wasn't the only one who knew it.

"Welcome." Win rose smoothly, his graciousness belied by the dark, suspicious expression in his eyes. He gestured to a leather chair in front of his gleaming desk. "Have a seat."

The secretary silently withdrew, shutting the door behind her.

Hannah shook her head. "Thank you, I prefer to stand."

"As you wish."

"I got your summons," she said coolly.

His mouth twitched, and he sat down, eyeing her. He was wearing a white shirt, its sleeves rolled up to mid-forearm, its top button undone, and had loosened his tie. Very sexy. His suit jacket was slung on a credenza to his right. His jaw looked even squarer than usual, but if Hannah could change only one thing about him, it would be his eyes. She'd fade them out, water them up a little, add some dark shadows and red lines. That done, surely the rest of him wouldn't seem nearly as appealing . . . or as dangerous.

"So," she said, crossing her arms over her chest, "who am I?"

"Hannah Marsh, the biographer."

She shrugged, neither confirming nor denying, but her heart was pounding. The man was relentless. But at least by leaving the Martha Washington biography for her, he'd given her fair warning of just what he knew.

He pushed a slender volume across his immaculate desk. It was her biography of three women married to famous robber barons of the nineteenth century. Like the study of Martha Washington, it had not been a bestseller. Win Harling would have had to dig to find her out.

"Okay," Hannah said unapologetically, "so I lied. In my position, wouldn't you have done the same?"

He made no apparent attempt to disguise his outright skepticism. After their rocky start, he was going to have a tough time believing anything she said. "Just what is your position?"

"Simply put, I'm a Marsh in Harling territory."

"There are just two Harlings in Boston." His tone was even and controlled, and all the more scathing for it. "My eighty-year-old uncle and me. Neither of us was disposed to harm or impede you in any way."

Hannah duly noted his use of the past tense. She decided she should keep her mouth shut until he finished.

Win sprang up and came around his desk, black walnut from the looks of it. Expensive. The man did know how to make money. "In my position, what would *you* do?"

She shrugged. "Leave me alone."

A smile, not an amiable one, tugged at the corners of his mouth. Hannah pushed aside the memory of that whisper of a kiss the other night.

"Wouldn't you want to find out what a woman posing as a member of your family was up to?" he asked. "Especially given the history between our two families."

"A lowly biographer? Nope. I wouldn't waste my time with her."

His eyes narrowed. In her mind, she washed out his black lashes. It didn't help. She still had to contend with the black irises.

"Wouldn't you think your behavior suspicious?" he asked.

"I'm not of a suspicious nature." She tilted her chin at him, unintimidated. They were fourteen floors up, in a well-guarded building. What could he do to her? "I'm a Marsh, remember? I don't think like a Harling."

He moved forward, so that they were only inches apart. She could smell his clean, expensive cologne and see a tiny scar at the corner of his right eye. It did not detract from the intensity of his gaze. "You're working on a biography of Priscilla Marsh."

"So?"

"So it's a nice cover for what you're really after."

"The Harling Collection," she said calmly. "I don't know what nefarious purpose you have attributed to me, but I only want to examine it for research purposes. I want to do as thorough a job as possible on Priscilla Marsh's life. Examining the Harling Collection could be very helpful in understanding Cotton Harling's thinking when he had her hanged."

Cotton's descendant stared at her in dubious silence. It was outrageous, Hannah thought, how sexy she found him. What would Priscilla have thought?

"That's the truth," she continued. "I didn't know it was even rumored to exist until I'd arrived in Boston and started doing my research, identifying myself as a Harling so I wouldn't arouse suspicion and might get better treatment. When I came here the other day, I tried to get in to see you without giving a name. I wanted to talk to you about my research first and explain. Of course, I thought you were your uncle. I had no idea..." She took a breath and glanced at him. "You don't get it, do you?"

"Oh, I get it. Your devious plan backfired."

She scowled. "No, you don't get it. You think I'm up to no good and I'm telling you I'm not. I was just doing my best under difficult circumstances."

"Of your own making. How do you explain the dress?"

"That was personal," she snapped. "I owed you for hunting me down like a dog."

His mouth twitched again, and this time she was sure he wanted to smile. At what? *She* wasn't having any fun.

She reached into her pocket and produced the check, by now wrinkled, she'd written on Saturday night, and thrust it at him. She could still return the dress, but she'd included its price in her check. "Here, take it. It's reimbursement for the lunch, the dress, the dinner, the donation to the New England Athenaeum—everything."

"I don't want your money, Hannah."

"Then what do you want?"

His eyes darkened and she stopped breathing. *Stupid question, Hannah. Stupid, stupid.* His answer was obvious in the heat of his gaze, the tenseness of his body.

What he wanted was her.

Just as she wanted him.

Their physical attraction was a fact, unpleasant, distracting, constant. And just as there was nothing they could do about their relationship to Cotton Harling and Priscilla Marsh, there was nothing they could do about the primitive longing that had erupted between them.

Well, Hannah thought, there was something....

But that was crazy. He was a Harling. He was the enemy. She couldn't think about going to bed with him!

Did he know that was what she was thinking? Could he even guess it?

"Okay, okay, fine," she said quickly, before he could respond. "Have it your way."

She spun around, preparing to leave. Wanting to leave. She would return to Marlborough Street, talk to Jonathan Harling about the Harling Collection, and bypass his know-it-all nephew altogether.

She got almost to the door before Win said, "The Harling Collection has been missing for at least a hundred years. Uncle Jonathan insists a Marsh stole it, just like a Marsh stole our land in southern Maine. Marsh Point, you call it now."

Stole Marsh Point? Damn, Cousin Thackeray! He must have known that was what the Harlings thought.

"Of all the—" Hannah whipped around, even more furious when she saw Win sitting calmly on the edge of his desk, watching her, waiting for her reaction. She pounded over to him, slinging her satchel. "That's what you think? That we've had the damned collection all along? Then why in hell would I risk life and limb trying to get in to see you to talk you into giving me access to it?"

"You tell me."

She groaned, itching to knock him off his high horse.

"So, you no longer deny that you're a Marsh," he said, rising.

It wasn't a question, but she said, "I never did deny it. I just didn't acknowledge it."

He touched her hair, wild from her mad dash across Boston, from the wind, from her anger. She fought the tingling sensation it caused. "A direct descendant of Priscilla Marsh?"

"The last."

He tucked a stray lock of hair behind her ear, letting his finger trace the outline of her jaw and creating a heat in her like none she'd known before. Then he dropped his hand to his side. "You're not from Ohio."

"I'm not from anywhere. I live in Maine now."

"Marsh Point."

"We didn't steal it." Her reply was based more out of loyalty to her cousin than on any certain knowledge.

"We have a case, you know. I've been looking into it. If we can prove the Marshes stole our deed, we can establish our right to the land." He remained close to her. "Until you showed up, I never paid much attention to Harling family history."

Hannah thought of Cousin Thackeray, who had been born on Marsh Point and wanted to die there. It was his home. Had he tried to talk Hannah out of going to Boston out of fear that she would rekindle the Harlings' claim to his slice of Maine?

Now Win Harling was on the case.

Thanks to her.

She faced him squarely. "What do you want from me?"

She saw the immediate spark of desire in his eyes and held her breath, wondering if he could see it mirrored in hers. But he didn't touch her, didn't act on the sexual tension hissing between them like a downed and very dangerous electrical wire. Neither did she.

"All I want," he said, "is the truth."

"I've told you everything I know." Her voice was hoarse; she paused to clear her throat. She wondered if his uncle had been filling him with the same kind of nasty tales about the Marshes that Cousin Thackeray had told her about the Harlings. "I understand you have no reason to trust me, but I'm not here to reignite the Marsh-Harling hostility. I'm just doing my work."

"If I knew you better, maybe I'd find it easier to believe you."

She tried to ignore the sudden softness of his voice. The fox coaxing the chickens to open the henhouse door. "Does your uncle know about me?"

"He suspects you're a Marsh, but that's all."

"He won't approve of my writing Priscilla's story, will he?"

"I'm sure he'll question your objectivity."

"Do you think he knows what happened to the Harling Collection, if it ever existed?"

Win smiled. "If he does, he'd never tell a Marsh."

She hoisted her satchel onto her shoulder, preparing once more to leave. She'd see what Jonathan Harling knew and didn't know, and what she could talk him into doing. "Truce?"

"Cease-fire. I'll talk to Uncle Jonathan this afternoon." Win stared at her for a moment. "Dinner tonight?"

It was more a challenge than an invitation. Hannah felt her throat tighten, but nodded. "Okay."

"You're not staying at any hotel in Boston," he said. She assumed he remembered the address she had given the cabdriver after the fund-raising dinner.

"No, I borrowed a friend's apartment on Pinckney Street, right around the corner from you."

His eyes held her. "So we are neighbors."

"I guess so," she said cheerfully and fled, wondering what she had got herself into. Why hadn't she listened to Cousin Thackeray to begin with and steered clear of Boston altogether?

"WIN HARLING KNOWS everything," Hannah told Cousin Thackeray from the kitchen phone. Her nerve endings were still on fire from her encounter with the wealthy Bostonian. She tried not to think of him simply as Win. That was too . . . personal.

Cousin Thackeray sniffed. "I told you this would happen."

"So you did."

"You coming home?"

"Not yet. Thackeray, what do you know about a Harling claim to Marsh Point?"

Silence.

"Thackeray?"

"They don't have one."

"Not a legitimate one, I'm sure. But—"

"But nothing's ever settled with a Harling," he grumbled, half under his breath. "Win Harling's after my land?"

"I don't think so. He says he doesn't know much about Harling family history, so all this stuff's fresh for him. He could laugh it off, or he could decide to take up the Harling cause. I just want you to be prepared." Not, she thought, that her dear cousin had paid her the same favor.

Cousin Thackeray laughed without amusement. "I'm always prepared for a Harling."

Hannah wished she could say the same for herself.

HOURS AFTER Hannah Marsh had left his office, Win was still trying to get her out of his mind. He walked home, hoping for distraction. The gusting wind, the traffic, the bustle of rush hour.

Nothing worked.

He made his way to Tremont Street off Boston Common, walking past the shaded grounds of Old Granary Burial Ground behind the First Congregational Church. Established in 1660, it was one of New England's oldest cemeteries. Thin, fragile, rectangular headstones stood at odd angles. Paul Revere was buried here, John Hancock, Samuel Adams, Ben Franklin's parents, the victims of the Boston Massacre.

And the man who had condemned Priscilla Marsh to death, Judge Cotton Harling.

He continued across Boston Common, welcoming its green grass and fluttering pigeons, its history. He crossed Charles Street and went through the Public Garden, where tulips and daffodils were in bloom. He didn't stop until he was in Back Bay, on Marlborough Street, letting himself into his uncle's brownstone with his key.

The door to his uncle's first-floor apartment was slightly ajar. Win creaked it halfway open. "Uncle Jonathan?"

He tensed when no response came.

Although Uncle Jonathan was not paranoid about city life, he was cautious and consistent about his personal security. He would never just step out for a quick walk and leave his door ajar, never mind unlocked. Had he been on his way out and stepped back inside because he'd forgotten something?

"Uncle Jonathan," Win called, raising his voice.

Still no response.

He went inside the apartment; its faded elegance made him feel as if he were taking a step back in time. Not wanting to startle his uncle, who might just be fine, Win shut the door hard and called him again as he headed from the small entry into the living room. Its bow windows looked onto Marlborough, and its Victorian style contrasted with the earlier Federal Period architecture of Beacon Hill.

"Good God!"

The place was a wreck.

Sofa cushions, drawers, shelves, the antique secretary; everything had been pulled out, tossed, scattered and left.

Win's heart pounded. *"Uncle Jonathan!"*

He leaped over books and magazines and papers and pounded down the short hall to his uncle's two bedrooms and bath.

Jonathan Harling was sitting on the edge of his fourposter bed, staring at the small fireplace. He looked unharmed, if gray-faced and stunned. He rubbed a hand through his thin hair and peered at his nephew. "I heard you."

Win squatted beside the old man. "Are you all right?"

His blue eyes focused on Win, betraying not fear, but anger. "She could have asked."

"What?"

"Your Hannah Marsh. She could have asked. I'd have told her no one's seen hide nor hair of the Harling Collection since around 1892."

Win jumped to his feet, stifling a rush of anger. He wanted to go out and track down Hannah and wring the truth out of her beautiful, lying lips. But he resisted the temptation. He had his uncle to see to. "Come on, Uncle Jonathan. I'll make you some tea and we'll talk. You're sure you're all right?"

"Oh, yes. I came in after the damage was done. Nearly had a damned heart attack on the spot. Wouldn't that have delighted the Marshes no end?" He reached for his cane, which lay on the bed, and used it to pull himself upright. He appeared, indeed, remarkably steady. "They'll never be satisfied until they've killed off one of us, the way they say we killed off Priscilla."

"Uncle . . ."

He shook his cane at Win. "She's a witch, I tell you!"

"Are you saying Hannah trashed your apartment looking for the Harling Collection?"

"Now you're getting it."

Win indulged his uncle's crotchety mood, given the scare the old man had just had, not to mention the circumstantial evidence that appeared to point to her. "Did you see her?"

"Nope. She's too clever by far for that. But I called the neighbors upstairs. They saw her. I gave them a description. She's easy to spot, you know."

Win knew.

"They said she came by this morning while I was at the club."

"Have you called the police?"

"Nope." He shook his head and pointed his cane again at Win. "This is between her and us Harlings."

Leaving it at that for the moment, Win helped his uncle, who kept grumbling he didn't need any damned help, into the kitchen, which had been spared the upheaval of the other rooms. Win filled a kettle with water and put it on the old gas stove.

Uncle Jonathan sat at his little gateleg table and heaved a long sigh. "And such a pretty woman to be such a scurrilous thief. I thought she was the one for you, Win, Marsh or no Marsh. Those eyes of hers . . . well, I should have known. She's got nothing but larceny in her heart."

"I'm having dinner with her tonight."

"Good. You can fleece the truth out of her."

Win thought he already had. He pictured Hannah Marsh standing in his office, proud, indignant, sexy, a woman to be reckoned with, who wouldn't project her own insecurities onto him. She hadn't looked as if she'd just ransacked an old man's apartment.

But then, what did he know about the real Hannah Marsh? She had already proved herself capable of lying and scheming to get her way, no matter how honorable her cause or understandable her reasoning. If indeed they were honorable and understandable. He had only her word to go on.

The kettle whistled, and Win made his uncle a pot of tea and even had a cup himself, though he was not a tea drinker.

"We need to talk," he said. "Then I'll clean up the place."

"Don't cancel with Miss Marsh on my account."

"Oh, no." He regarded his uncle's pale face with growing anger. What was worth terrifying an eighty-year-old man? "I'll keep our date on your account."

Uncle Jonathan grinned feebly. "That's the spirit."

HANNAH SIPPED at the glass of wine that Win had poured her and watched him whisk together raspberry vinegar and olive oil for the mixed green salad he'd thrown together. She hadn't expected dinner would be at his house. "What?" she'd asked upon entering the historic Beacon Hill mansion. "No maids?"

Win had smiled over his shoulder. "No furniture, either."

He wasn't exaggerating by much. Although the place retained its regal lines and potential, it needed work. Win Harling clearly could afford to have it done. Why didn't he?

There was a lot, Hannah admitted, she didn't know about the man. A lot mere prejudice couldn't explain.

"I haven't been here that long—I wanted the house back in the family and snapped it up when I had the chance. I keep thinking I'd like to do the work myself, but I haven't gotten around to it."

He swirled the contents of the glass carafe, then added pinches of dried herbs from small unmarked containers. "How do you know what's what?" Hannah asked.

"Who says I do?"

A seat-of-the-pants cook. "Dinner should be interesting."

"Always."

The kitchen was large and drafty, this morning's dark clouds now pouring forth a cold, steady rain. Expecting a restaurant, Hannah had put on a simple dress and flats. Now she wished she'd brought a sweater.

"You're shivering," Win observed.

"Not really."

He pulled off his cardigan and tossed it to her. "Here, put this on."

"Won't you get cold?"

"Nope. Cooking always makes me hot." He had his back to her, but Hannah didn't need to see his expression to guess what he was thinking.

The sweater was old but bulky, a thick, cotton knit still warm from his body. She slipped it on. He was wider through the torso than she was, and his arms were longer. She pushed up the sleeves, the fabric soft and well-worn, like a caress against her skin. She licked her lips, suddenly feeling self-conscious, even somewhat aroused. Wearing his sweater was too much like having him hold her. Dinner maybe hadn't been a good idea, but she had to find out what he knew—what he intended to do—about Marsh Point. If anything. She'd stirred up this trouble; she'd see to it that it didn't reach Cousin Thackeray.

Win glanced back at her. "Better?"

"Yes."

He did not, she observed, look the least bit chilly himself in his close-fitting jeans and dark purple, short-sleeved pullover. She would bet it wasn't just the cooking that kept him warm, or even his all too apparent physical desire for her. There was also the fact that they were in his house, his city, on his turf. Easy for him to stay nice and toasty.

"What did you do today?" he asked casually.

"Not much. I spent most of the morning at the New England Athenaeum, met you, then headed up to the Boston Public Library. After that I went back to the apartment and entered my notes into my laptop."

Win got a small paper bag from the refrigerator and withdrew from it a mound of fresh linguine, which he promptly dropped into a pot of bubbling water. He scooped a cupful of the boiling water into a plain white pasta dish and swirled it around while the linguine cooked. "You didn't happen to wander over to Marlborough Street, did you?"

"Mmm . . . why would I?"

"I don't know." He stopped what he was doing and regarded her, his expression hard, challenging. "Why would you?"

Hannah licked her lips. "Am I being set up here?"

"Just tell the truth, Hannah."

"All right. I found your uncle Jonathan's address this morning in the rare book room. Before answering your summons, I took a walk over to Marlborough Street."

"Why?"

"To talk to him about the Harling Collection. I thought he'd know more than you would, and that he might be more reasonable than you would."

"Did you see him?"

"No, he wasn't in."

"How do you know?"

"What do you mean, how do I know? I rang his doorbell and he didn't answer. I assumed he wasn't home."

"Then you didn't go into his apartment?"

"No."

"What about this afternoon? Did you go back to Marlborough Street?"

She shook her head. "I decided to wait until we'd talked before trying to see your uncle again."

Win didn't say a word. Instead he picked up the bubbling pot and dumped the contents into a colander in the sink, steam enveloping him. He set down the empty pot. Hannah noticed the muscles in his back and upper arms, felt the raw sexiness of the man. Her careful preparations for dealing with the Harlings of Boston had been way off the mark.

He transferred the pasta to the warmed dish, then spooned on a herb and oil sauce and sautéed vegetables, tossing them with two forks.

"Why the interrogation?" Hannah finally asked.

"Because I don't know you." He brought the bowls of pasta and salad to the table, which wasn't set for dinner. "I don't know you at all, Hannah Marsh."

Suddenly he turned and lifted her by the elbows, slipping his hands under the heavy sweater and drawing her toward him. She didn't resist. To maintain her balance she let her palms press against his chest. It was even harder than she had anticipated. He drew her even closer, until she had little choice but to let her arms slide around his back. Now her breasts were pressed against his chest. She could feel the nipples turning into small pebbles. How much more of this could she stand?

How much more did she want?

Their eyes locked, just for an instant. She knew what he wanted. What she wanted.

Then his mouth closed over hers, hot and hungry, his tongue urged her lips apart, as if its probing would find all her secrets, answer all his questions. She felt herself responding. Her mind said she was crazy. He was a Harling, Cousin Thackeray had warned her, but her body didn't care. Her tongue did its own probing, its own urging. Her breasts strained against the muscles of his chest. He pushed one knee between her legs, pressing his hard masculinity against her, kneading her hips until she moaned softly, agonizingly, into his mouth. *Don't stop,* her body said, over and over. *Don't ever stop.*

But he took her by the shoulders and disentangled himself, pulling himself away. She felt swollen, frustrated, a little embarrassed. She couldn't read his expression. His eyes were masked, dark and mesmerizing.

"Did you ransack my uncle's apartment?" he asked hoarsely.

"What?"

"You heard me."

"No, I—of course I didn't!"

"You never went back to Marlborough Street?"

"I said no. What happened? Is your uncle all right?"

"Someone broke into his apartment. He's shaken up but otherwise fine."

She stepped back, increasing the physical and psychic distance between them. "So that's what this is about. You're trying to weaken my defenses and get me to admit to something I didn't do. Well, you're way off base, Win Harling. I've told you the truth."

He nodded curtly. "Fair enough." He picked up the two bowls that stood on the table. "We'll eat in the dining room."

"I don't know how I can have dinner with you after— My God, I can't believe you'd think I could rob an old man!"

"Why not? Think of all the things you believe I'm capable of doing." He grinned at her over his shoulder. "Come on, Hannah. My doubts about you aren't upsetting you nearly as much as that kiss."

She grew cool. "I've been kissed before."

"But have you ever responded like that?"

It was only nominally a question. He had got it into his head that she hadn't. That he'd been the first man she'd let get to her like that with a first kiss. The problem was, he was right. Ordinarily she held back. Deliberately, easily. She had never before permitted herself to respond with such abandon, such openness.

A serious mistake, perhaps?

Well, what was done was done. He had used her. Manipulated her. Lowered her defenses so that he could pose his nasty question and catch her off guard. He hadn't been anywhere close to out of control.

But he had been aroused. No doubt about that.

As he led her down a short hall, she noticed its cherry floor needed sanding. They entered a chandeliered dining room with the ugliest wallpaper she'd ever seen. Parts of it had been peeled back, revealing a clashing, but prettier, paper underneath. The only furnishings were an antique grandfather clock, a massive, gorgeous, cherry table and a couple of folding, metal chairs that decidedly didn't match. The walls were wainscoted and the ceilings high, the windows looking onto a darkened courtyard. The table was set with cloth place mats and simple white porcelain plates.

"I'll get the wine," Win said and disappeared.

Alone in the dining room, Hannah took the opportunity to restore her composure. She wiped her still-sensitized mouth with a soft cloth napkin and listened to the ticking of the grandfather clock, letting it soothe her. Although the Harling House was in the middle of the city, it might have been on Marsh Point itself for all its quiet and sense of isolation, its potential for loneliness.

Suddenly she wondered if she and Win Harling had more in common than either wanted to admit. Perhaps what had them groping for each other wasn't just a physical attraction gone overboard, but a subconscious understanding of that commonality.

He returned with their two glasses and the bottle of wine.

"I should go," she said.

"I know. I should make you go." He refilled her glass. "But there's another matter we need to discuss."

She could think of several. "What's that?"

"A rare copy of the Declaration of Independence, possibly worth hundreds of thousands of dollars."

6

"I DON'T KNOW what you're talking about," Hanna said simply.

Win lighted two tall, slender, white candles and sa on the folding chair at one end of the table, watchin her in the flickering light. She was, he thought, a be witching woman. "I figured that was what you'd say.

"It's the truth."

"Tell me," he said, pausing to sip his wine. "How di you learn about the Harling Collection?"

"It was mentioned in passing in something I read. can't remember offhand exactly what it was, but I kee exhaustive records. I could look it up."

"Why don't you?"

"I don't like your tone, Mr. Harling." Hers was as sertive, bordering on angry. "And I'm not under an obligation to obey any orders from you."

He set down his wineglass and passed her the past bowl, noting the slenderness of her wrists, the unsel conscious femininity of her movements. "Tell me agai why you want to get your hands on the Harling Co lection."

"I don't want to 'get my hands' on it. I want access it—a chance to study it for anything it might contai pertinent to my work."

"Meaning anything on Priscilla Marsh or Cotton Harling."

"That's right."

"Then you're saying you didn't realize the Harling Collection is rumored to include a valuable, rare copy of the Declaration of Independence."

He could see his words sinking in, along with all their ramifications, and was suddenly glad they'd kissed before he'd brought up the touchy subject.

"Oh, I see what you're getting at." She bit off each word, anger visibly boiling to the surface. Her green eyes were hot, almost liquid. "You're accusing me of breaking into your uncle's apartment in an attempt to find the Harling Collection or some clue as to its location, in order to steal this Declaration of Independence and make a handy profit for myself at Harling expense."

Win scooped pasta onto her plate, and then onto his, maintaining his calm. "Only Uncle Jonathan doesn't know where the Harling Collection is. No one does. No one can even verify it exists, or ever did." His gaze fell upon her; it would be easier if she weren't so damned attractive. "Unless you have a new lead you're keeping to yourself."

She gave him a haughty look. "Why would you think that?"

He shrugged. "You're a scholar. You're good at doing research. Who knows what you might have ferreted out in the last week?"

"We're in quite a position, aren't we?"

Her voice rasped with not very well-suppressed fury, although, given her behavior this past week, Win couldn't understand why she was so irritated. Under the circumstances, he felt his suspicions were quite natural.

"By pretending to be a Harling," she went on, speaking tightly, "I shattered any trust you might have had in me, no matter how innocuous my intentions or how understandable my reasons. You still can't believe me. Won't believe me. Then there's the impact of three centuries of Marsh-Harling conflict...."

"It hasn't had any impact on me." Win tried his pasta; not bad. Hannah might calm down if she ate some. "Maybe it's had an impact on you, but not on me. I was hardly even aware of the extent of the grudge you Marshes hold against us."

"You're a Harling...."

"But not a Bostonian. I was born and raised in New York. I only came to Boston last year, when I bought this house and moved my offices."

She didn't seem particularly interested in his personal history, but he found himself wondering about hers. Where did Hannah Marsh live? How? And what made her tick?

"You had to know about Cotton and Priscilla," she said.

He smiled. "You talk about them as if you know them."

"That's my job, to feel as if I know the people I write about. It's pure arrogance to believe I do, but I have at least to have some sense of who they were. I have to feel hat if they suddenly came to life in my kitchen, I'd recognize them." She caught herself and took a breath. "Not that I have to explain myself to you."

"Of course not. Yes, I was aware of Cotton and Priscilla, but I haven't participated in perpetuating three-hundred-year-old grudges."

"Well, aren't you high and mighty? I've been doing everything I can to maintain my objectivity. I don't have a personal grudge against the Harlings. And if you don't have anything against the Marshes, why check into your family's absurd claim to Marsh Point?"

"It's not absurd," he said offhandedly. "Actually, it's rather well-founded."

Her look would have shot holes in him if it could have. "There, you see? You're no saint, Win Harling."

"Oh," he said playfully, "that I'm definitely not."

He could see her recognizing his words as the multipronged threat he'd intended them to be. Even with the pasta and more wine, he could still taste her mouth, imagine the taste of her skin.

"The point is," she said a little hoarsely, "where do we go from here?"

His gaze held her. In the old, candlelit room, she could have passed for her doomed ancestor. But Win couldn't make up for the wrongs of Cotton Harling. He had his uncle to consider. "Trust is earned."

Hannah sprang to her feet, visibly indignant. "I didn't break into your uncle's apartment. I had no idea until tonight the Harling Collection might include anything of monetary value." She threw down her napkin, resisting an impulse, Win thought, to try to whip his head off with it. "There's nothing I can do to make you believe me. I'm not even going to try. Good night, Win. Please tell your uncle I hope he's all right.'

And that was that.

Off she stomped to the front door, yanking it open and slamming it shut on her way out.

An angry woman, Hannah Marsh.

She hadn't eaten so much as a pea pod of her dinner. Win sighed and got up. He supposed he ought to go after her and apologize. But for what?

And what bothered her more? he wondered. His accusing her of breaking and entering or kissing her? Wanting her as much and as obviously as he did?

How the hell was he supposed to know for sure what she was up to? His first loyalty was to Uncle Jonathan, not to some fair-haired scholar with a bee in her bonnet about his ancestors.

Yet Hannah Marsh was so much more. He sensed it, knew it. There was a depth and complexity to her he hadn't even begun to probe.

He gritted his teeth at the unbidden thought of just how much of Ms. Marsh he wanted to probe....

"Damn," he muttered. Now it was his turn to throw down his napkin and pound from the room. He'd lost his appetite.

The doorbell rang.

"Hannah?"

He headed for the entry and pulled open the heavy front door, only to find his elderly uncle leaning on his cane and looking none the worse for wear for his day's ordeal. Without preamble the old man said, "The damned thief did get away with something."

"What? You don't have much of value...."

"Anne Harling's diary."

Win stared. Now what? "Who the hell's Anne Harling?"

"Your great-great-aunt, remember? The one who gathered together the Harling Collection. She died in 1892."

Wonderful. "Uncle Jonathan..."

"Invite me in, Winthrop. We need to talk."

THE NEXT MORNING, Hannah arrived at the New England Athenaeum within five minutes of its opening and asked to see Preston Fowler, in private. He brought her into his office, where she admitted to him that she was not Hannah Harling of the Ohio Harlings.

"I'm a Marsh," she said baldly.

He paled.

"Hannah Marsh."

"The biographer?"

At least he'd heard of her. She nodded.

He sighed, looking slightly ill. "My, my."

"I'm sorry I lied to you. It was just an expedient. I didn't think I could use the facilities here if you knew I was a Marsh." She swallowed. "I didn't think you'd risk offending the Harlings."

Fowler winced. "Your two families...the Harlings and the Marshes..."

"The history between us hasn't affected—and won't affect—my work," she said crisply, trying to sound like

the professional she was. "I didn't want my being a
Marsh to come into play. Hence my ruse. I'm very
sorry."

"Oh, dear."

"The Harlings know the truth now, and I've made it
clear to them that you were in no way a party to my de-
ceit." She sounded so stuffy and contrite, but in fact she
was neither. What she wanted to do was tell Win Harling to go to hell and Preston Fowler to have a little more
integrity than to suck up to rich Bostonians for dona-
tions. "That's all I came to say."

Fowler tilted back his chair, placing the tips of his
fingers together to make a tent. He sighed again. "How
awkward."

"It's not awkward, Mr. Fowler. Not at all. I'm leaving Boston today. All you have to do is carry on with
your work and pretend I never existed."

He nodded. "Very well. What about your biography
of Priscilla? Will it go forward now that this has happened?"

"Of course. Why shouldn't it? Most of my research
is completed."

"But the Harlings . . ."

Hannah sat forward. "I don't care what the Harlings
want or think."

With that she apologized once more, assured him no
harm had been done to his venerable institution and
headed out. Yesterday's clouds and rain had been
pushed off over the Atlantic, leaving blue sky and
warm air in their wake. Hannah breathed in deep
lungfuls of it before crossing the Public Garden and

utting past the Ritz Carlton Hotel into Boston's Back
ay, straight for Marlborough Street.

Jonathan Harling asked for her name twice over the
ntercom. "Marsh," she said both times. "It's Hannah
Marsh."

He buzzed her in, anyway.

"Come on in," he said, opening his apartment door.
I've been wondering when you'd show up. Think the
oof'll cave in with a Marsh and Harling under it?
Though I suppose if it didn't last night, with you and
Vin, we should be all right."

The glitter in his eye suggested—although Hannah
ouldn't be certain—he had a fair idea that she and his
ephew had more than simply shared the same roof.
ut she had vowed to stop thinking about Win's mouth
n hers, his hard maleness thrust against her. She would
ot be at the mercy of her hormones.

Nonetheless, every fiber of her body—of her be-
ng—said she wanted more from Jonathan's nephew
han a kiss, more than a heady embrace. She wanted
o feel his skin against hers, his maleness inside her.

She wanted him to make love to her . . . with her.

There was no point in denying the obvious. Her
brupt departure last night had had less to do with his
isgusting suspicion—his talk of the Declaration of In-
ependence and of larceny—than with her ongoing,
nstoppable, outrageous physical response to him. His
ark, penetrating gaze had filled her with erotic no-
ions. His hands, as he'd lighted the candles, had left her
reathless, conjured up images of his touch on her
nouth, her breasts, between her legs. Just looking at

him had made her think of the two of them together i
bed, or just right there on the dining room floor.

Such wild, irresponsible thinking had to stop.

It just had to. It was perverse to want a man sl
couldn't possibly have. A man who, even as her bod
ached for him, believed she was a thief, a grudg
holding Marsh, a woman he couldn't trust.

Jonathan Harling's apartment looked tidy, if clu
tered, no evidence of a thorough ransacking still a
parent. He offered Hannah a seat on an overstuffe
overly firm sofa. He himself flopped into a cushione
rocker. He was casually dressed, in a cardigan fraye
at the elbows and chinos that must have seen Harr
Truman into office. Hannah didn't feel the least bit o
of place in her leggings and giant Maine sweatshirt.

"What can I do for you?" Jonathan Harling asked

"I wanted to tell you how sorry I am about yeste
day. Win told me. I hope you know I wasn't involve
I—" She broke off awkwardly, then decided she mig
as well get on with it. "You know by now I'm a Mars
and there are no Ohio Harlings."

He grunted and waved a hand. "I knew that da
ago."

"Do you hate me for being a Marsh?"

"Nope. I don't trust you, but I don't hate you."

A fine distinction. Hannah let it pass.

"Be stupid to trust you," Jonathan added.

"I suppose, given the history of our two familie
that's not unreasonable. Also given my own behavio
I'm leaving Boston today—"

"Win know?"

She bristled. "Why should he?"

"I didn't say he should or shouldn't," the old man replied, matching her gruffness. "Just asked if he did."

"No. I haven't seen him since last night."

"You going to tell him?"

"I don't see any reason to tell your nephew anything, and I didn't come here to discuss him. I . . ." She frowned. "What are you looking at?"

"You. Trying to figure you out. How come you go all snot-nosed professor when someone asks you a personal question?"

"I'm not a professor."

He rocked back in his chair. "You and Win got something going?"

"Mr. Harling . . ."

"He threw me out last night after I started asking him personal questions. I do it all the time. Pride myself on being able to say anything I want to my own nephew, but I mentioned you, and out on my ear I went." He folded his scrawny hands in his lap. "Must be you two got something going."

Only Hannah's years of dealing with her exasperating Cousin Thackeray kept her from gaping at Jonathan Harling or throwing something at him. Or politely leaving. "Dr. Harling, I suspect your rather salty speech pattern is a total fake. You're a scholar yourself."

He waved a hand dismissively.

"Legal history. You taught at Harvard for fifty years."

"What, you writing a biography of me? I thought your only subjects were dead people."

She couldn't suppress a smile. "You're not dead yet."

"Glad you noticed."

"Look, I just came by to tell you I had nothing to do with yesterday's break-in. I only wanted to look at the Harling Collection for research purposes. I didn't know it might include a valuable copy of the Declaration of Independence. And I'm going home." She climbed to her feet. "It's been interesting meeting you. Should I send you a copy of my biography of Priscilla Marsh when it comes out?"

He lifted his bony shoulders, clearly feigning disinterest. "If you remember."

"Oh, I'll remember."

She told him not to bother seeing her to the door, but halfway there she felt his presence behind her and spun around. He was leaning on his cane, alert, still handsome in his own way. "Will you be mentioning Anne Harling?"

"Who?"

"You heard me."

"Yes, I did, but I'm not familiar..." She paused, searching her memory. "Cotton Harling's brother was married to a woman named Anne, wasn't he? She died before Priscilla was executed, as I recall."

"I'm talking about my great-aunt."

Hannah frowned, uncertain where he was leading her.

"She never married. Lived in the Harling House on Louisburg Square until her death, late in the last century. Interesting woman. She's the one who supposedly gathered the family documents together into the Harling Collection."

"I see," Hannah said, although she didn't.

Jonathan smiled knowingly. "Her diary was stolen from this apartment yesterday."

His words only took a few seconds to penetrate. "Oh, my. And you think . . . it would seem logical that I . . ."

"That you stole it, yes."

"But I didn't."

"So you say."

"Win . . . Have you told your nephew?"

"Told him last night."

And he hadn't broken her door down at dawn to demand an explanation. Maybe he didn't care nearly as much about her supposedly larcenous tendencies as much as he claimed. Or maybe hadn't liked the idea of dragging her out of bed at the crack of dawn. With his blood boiling and hers about to boil, who knows where it would have lead?

"I thought perhaps that was why you were leaving town," Jonathan Harling said, looking decidedly smug.

Hannah threw back her shoulders. "It isn't."

"Win's not going to scare you off, eh?"

"Nobody will."

"Then you're going to stay?"

She felt Jonathan Harling's trap snap shut around her and knew all she could do was wriggle and complain. Or chew her leg off. Figuratively speaking. "You haven't left me any choice."

He grinned. "That was the whole idea."

WIN WAS WAITING, slouching against Hannah's apartment door, when she rounded the corner of Pinckney

Street. He could hear her sharp intake of breath when she spotted him. His own reaction was more under control; he'd had a few extra seconds to adjust to her imminent presence. He watched her slow down, saw a wariness creep into her gait. He also noticed how her hair tangled in the afternoon wind and glistened in the bright sun.

"I thought you'd be working," she said, coming closer.

"I left early."

"Is it costing you?"

He smiled. "In more ways than you probably would want to know."

"Try me."

Oh, lady, he thought. "I'd better resist. Let's just say I don't take many afternoons off. Mind if I come in?"

Without answering, she unlocked the heavy black door that led to the two basement apartments. The main entrance to the building was up the steps to their right, the first floor elevated, so that Hannah's borrowed apartment was almost at ground level. She unlocked that door, too. The apartment was predictably small, cluttered with her laptop computer, index cards, spiral notebooks, folders, papers, books.

"Look," she began, going straight into the kitchen area and filling a kettle with water, "if this is about Anne Harling's missing diary, I've already spoken to your uncle. He told me everything. I don't know what happened to it. I honestly don't. I didn't steal it."

"Did he tell you she was the one who gathered together the Harling Collection?"

She nodded, setting the kettle upon the stove. She dried her hands and headed back into the living area, where Win was clearly considering just where he might sit. Not one surface was free. She settled the matter for him, lifting a pile of folders from a chair and dropping them onto the floor. "Have a seat. Would you like tea?"

"No, thank you."

What a life she must lead, he thought, sitting down. Steeped in the past. Inundated with books, documents, paper. Did she have friends? Romances? Or was her strength the past, not the present? He wondered about her and men.

"I borrowed this place from a friend of mine. She's taking my cottage on Marsh Point sometime this summer." Hannah returned to the kitchen area, banging around as she pulled out a cup, saucer, strainer and teapot—anxious, he thought, to stay busy. "I can always stay with Cousin Thackeray if I can't get away when she wants the place."

"Who's he?"

"Thackeray Marsh. He reminds me somewhat of your Uncle Jonathan."

"Lucky you," Win said, amused.

She laughed. "Thackeray would hang me out to dry for saying that. He's not much on Harlings. But..." Her shoulders lifted, as if she couldn't quite express her feelings. "I owe him."

"For what?"

"Saving me."

And she yanked open the refrigerator, blocking Win's view of her. She had said more than she'd meant to.

More, certainly, than she felt he deserved to know. But it wasn't enough. He wanted to know more, everything.

"You're sure you don't want tea? I can make coffee, too. I have one of those one-cup drip things."

"I'm fine. Thanks. How did your cousin save you, Hannah?"

"After my mother died five years ago—my father was already dead—I found myself wanting to see Marsh Point, and I met him. He's a historian, too. He understood me, knew I needed roots, a place to belong." She shut the refrigerator door and glared at Win. "I won't let you take Marsh Point away from him."

He said nothing. Her relationship with her cousin, he sensed, was much like his own with his uncle. What else might they have in common?

She set about her tea making. Win hated the stuff himself, but any more coffee today and he'd spin off to the moon. After Hannah's abrupt departure last night and Uncle Jonathan's peculiar visit, Win had taken a long walk up and down the meandering streets of Beacon Hill, trying to piece his thoughts and feelings into some kind of rational whole. But there were too many variables, too many bizarre, uncontrollable longings. Back home, he'd slept for a couple of hours, but had been up again at dawn, making a pot of coffee, seeing Hannah Marsh with him in his kitchen, imagining them up together at dawn after a night of lovemaking. Wondering if she really was a lying thief.

"So why," she said thoughtfully, carrying her tea into the living area, "do you think Anne Harling's diary was stolen?"

"I don't know."

"Come on. You have a dozen reasons why you think I stole it. I presume that's why you're here, to interrogate me on the possibilities."

"I'm here to talk to you. That's all. No accusations, no offensive questions, just straightforward talk."

"We'll be logical and rational."

He ignored her sarcasm. "Right."

"Is that what you tell your clients? Let's be logical and rational about your financial portfolio'?"

"Sometimes. Other times logic and rationality aren't at issue. Emotion is, wants and needs that go to the heart of a client's being, what he or she is about, what makes them feel alive. Sometimes a client just needs my encouragement to go for the impulsive and outrageous."

"All in a day's work, I suppose," she said lightly, but he could see that his words had had an effect. Their kiss had been impulsive and maybe even outrageous. It was still on her mind, just as it was on his.

She dropped to the floor and sat cross-legged amid her scattered research materials. Uncle Jonathan's apartment hadn't looked much worse than this yesterday, after it had been ransacked. But she seemed relaxed enough, setting her cup and saucer upon an enormous dictionary, muttering something about computer dictionaries just not being the same, no comparison. She ran her fingers through her hair, working out several small tangles.

"If I were going to break into your uncle's apartment specifically to steal Anne Harling's diary," she said, "don't you think I'd have gone out of my way to make it look like a real robbery and stolen a bunch of other stuff?"

"Not necessarily. You might have thought Uncle Jonathan wouldn't miss the diary until too late, if at all. You might have thought he didn't even realize he had it."

"Quite a risk."

"Maybe, maybe not. If Uncle Jonathan did realize the diary was missing, he would assume the other things had been taken as a smoke screen. If you were going to get caught, better with just an old diary in your possession than the family silver, so to speak."

"The 'you' here being a hypothetical you, not me."

He smiled. "Of course."

"So the thief took a chance."

"Possibly."

"It's also possible, wouldn't you say, that the diary isn't missing, that your uncle got rid of it years ago, or maybe never had it to begin with and just forgot."

"Obviously you don't know Uncle Jonathan, but never mind. How do you explain the break-in?"

She shrugged. "He's on the first floor of a nice building. He, or someone else in his building, could have left the front door ajar, and our would-be thief took advantage. He got into your uncle's apartment, pulled the place apart, didn't find any ready cash or easily fenced valuables and took off, cutting his losses."

"Highly coincidental, don't you think?"

"Life is full of coincidences." She drank some of her tea, watching him over the rim of her cup. "What's so special about Anne Harling's diary?"

"Nothing, so far as I know. That's the point. It's what *you* think is special about it that's important." Win stretched his legs. "Suppose you believe it contains a clue as to what happened to the Harling Collection."

She shook her head. "Ridiculous. The Harlings being the Harlings, they'd have discovered the clue decades ago and skimmed off anything of value in the collection themselves."

"I can't argue with that. But maybe it's a clue you—"

"Our thief."

"As you wish. Maybe you're the only one who understands the significance of the clue."

"Pretty farfetched."

"But the risk of breaking into Uncle Jonathan's apartment would have to be worth the potential benefit. Don't you agree?"

"I still like my idea about it being a coincidence."

"That's because it lets you off the hook." Win rose and walked over to where she sat, looking so casual and honest with her cup of tea. So unselfconsciously sexy. He lifted a manila folder marked Puritan Hangings of the 1690s. Charming subject. "You've been steeping yourself in Marsh-Harling history for how long?"

"I began work on Priscilla's biography last September."

"And you've been in Boston over a week, immersing yourself in three centuries of history that you can feel and touch. You've traveled the same streets Priscilla Marsh traveled. You've seen what Cotton Harling's descendants have become."

She set her teacup upon the floor beside her, a slight tremble in her hand. "I don't know what you're getting at, but I'm a professional historian. I don't get emotionally involved in my subjects."

"You're human, Hannah," Win said softly, reaching out and touching her hair. "Your mother's mother's mother's mother. How far back does it go? Does it even matter? Priscilla Marsh was wrongly hanged, and here in Boston you've been immersed in that wrong. It would be understandable if you let yourself get carried away."

"Into ransacking an old man's apartment?"

"And other things," he said deliberately.

She wriggled her legs apart and shot up. She appeared ready to bolt. But there was nowhere to go. This was her apartment, her space. And he hadn't moved an inch. To get past him, she would have to leap over stacks of books and files, a fact he could see her assessing, processing.

"You can't run from what's going on between us," he said, hearing his voice outwardly calm but laced with tension, desire—and determination. "Neither can I."

"I'm going back to Maine," she blurted.

"I figured as much."

"If you want to search my things before I leave . . ."

"If you did take the diary, you'd be too smart to leave it here. You wouldn't risk my showing up and tearing apart the place until I found it."

"Was that your plan when you came here?"

She held her chin raised, haughty and unafraid—or at least she was trying to appear so. Her eyes gave her away. But she wasn't afraid of him. He could see that. She was afraid, he thought, only of herself, of their muddled feelings about each other, on top of the very clear, obvious and tenacious physical attraction between them. Emotions, not just overexcited hormones, were at work and at stake.

"No," he said. "This was."

He tucked one finger under her chin, giving her a chance to tell him to go to hell, but she didn't. He breathed deeply, knowing he was crazy. They both were.

"Hannah," he whispered, and closed his mouth over hers.

Her lips were smooth and soft and if not welcoming him, at least not turning him away. He tasted them. She tasted back.

"I wish I didn't want this to happen," she whispered into his mouth.

"I know."

But it was happening, and neither of them wanted it to stop. He pulled her to him, felt her hands around his middle, her slender body pressed against him. Her tongue slid into his mouth, tentatively at first, then more boldly. He could feel every fiber of him responding . . . aching . . . wanting. . . .

And then it was over.

He couldn't say if it was he or she who pulled back. He wasn't sure it mattered. He only knew that within too short a time he was back on Pinckney Street's brick sidewalk, looking at the Charles River in the distance and wondering what in blue hell had happened.

She had wanted him. He had wanted her.

So why the devil wasn't he in there, making love to Hannah Marsh?

He raked one hand through his hair and heaved a sigh. He hadn't been motivated by any false nobility or nebulous impression that making love to her wasn't, deep down, what she wanted, as well. And it sure as hell wasn't the missing diary of some aunt who'd been dead for a hundred years or his eccentric, crotchety old uncle that had stopped him.

It was, he thought, very simple.

He was falling for Hannah Marsh and didn't want to make a wrong move.

And right now, taking into account not only the history that had brought them to this moment but all he didn't know about this woman, who could seem so outrageous and cocky one minute and so prim and proper the next, scooping her up and carting her off to bed would be a mistake. Never mind how much he wanted it. Never mind how much she wanted it.

First things first, he told himself. First he had to learn more about Hannah Priscilla Marsh. Find out what made her tick. Then...

By God, he thought. Then there'd be no stopping him.

"YOU'RE HOME EARLY," Thackeray said when Hannah reported in upon her return to southern Maine. "I knew your common sense would prevail."

She smiled. "It wasn't common sense, it was self-preservation."

"Whatever works."

When Hannah looked at her elderly cousin, she couldn't help but think of Jonathan Harling in Boston. On the surface all the two old men had in common was their age, but Hannah suspected they were much more similar deep down than either would care to admit.

He shoved a cat off the chair near the fire in his front room. It was cold, dank and foggy on Marsh Point, but Hannah had already been out to the rocks and tasted the ocean. She was home.

While she had a small winterized cottage close to the water's edge, Thackeray had a bona fide house, built in 1880, with high ceilings, leaded glass windows and four fireplaces. His wife, a native of Maine, had died ten years ago and they'd had no children, but still he'd managed to clutter up the place. He persisted in subscribing to a dozen magazines, plus *The Wall Street Journal* and *The New York Times*. He refused to read any of the Boston papers, lest he run across the Harling name, be it a reference to a live one or a dead one. Boston, he maintained, had never been kind to the Marsh family.

"Tea?" he offered.

"No, thank you. I just wanted to say hi."

"Anything to report?"

She decided not to tell him she had kissed a Harling, but filled him in on everything else, including the two Jonathan Winthrop Harlings' suspicion that she was after the rumored copy of the Declaration of Independence. Cousin Thackeray snorted at the very idea. She laughed, appreciating his unconditional support. But it had always been there, as consistent as the tide.

"What're you going to do now?" he asked.

Exorcise Win Harling from my mind....

"Start writing, I guess," she said, hating the note of melancholy in her voice. Her life would never be the same after Boston and her brush with the Harlings. "I've done more than enough research to get started, at least. I can't help but feel I ran away from Boston, but I hope that will pass."

"You exercised good judgment, that's all. You didn't run away from a thing."

No, not from a thing. From Win.

"You're not the type," Cousin Thackeray added, clearly convinced, as always, that any Marsh who deliberately avoided a Harling was just doing the right thing.

Hannah wished she shared his certainty. Instead she could only think about the desire Win Harling stirred up in her with his kisses, his touch, his very presence.

And it was not just a matter of physical desire. In spite of their differences, she had felt an emotional connection starting to grow between them, something beyond flaming hormones.

But staying had become impossible. She simply hadn't been willing to risk the Harlings finding some way to blame her for Jonathan's ransacked apartment and the missing Anne Harling diary. She couldn't risk reigniting their outrage over having lost their beautiful point in southern Maine to a Marsh. She couldn't risk their finding some loophole—and Win was just the high-minded, bulldog type to find one—that would put it back in their hands.

She couldn't risk falling in love with Win Harling.

She shook her head. No. She really couldn't. She had her work. It would fill her mind, once she got into it.

"Hannah?"

Smiling, she kissed her cousin on the cheek and patted his hand. "It's good to be back."

UNCLE JONATHAN had spread a detailed map of Maine on Win's table when he arrived home from work, the evening after Hannah Marsh bolted. It was after eight. He could see his uncle had helped himself to the leftovers of the aborted dinner. The old man had also polished off the last of the wine.

"Trying to drown your sorrows in work, eh?" Uncle Jonathan said, cocking his head at his nephew.

Win slung his suit coat over the back of a folding chair. "I had to catch up on a few things."

"Distracting woman, that Hannah Marsh. If I didn't know better, I'd say old Cotton offed her ancestor, just so he could get his mind back on track."

"That's ridiculous," Win said.

"Of course it is, but if Priscilla Marsh looked anything like your Hannah, she made one hell of a Puritan." Uncle Jonathan abruptly turned his attention back to his map, running one finger down Maine's jagged coastline. "There's another helping of that anemic spaghetti in the refrigerator."

"Thanks, but I'm not hungry."

"Going to starve yourself over a woman?"

Win sighed. "I had a late lunch with a client. Uncle Jonathan, what are you doing here?"

"Besides acquainting myself with the pitiful existence you endure here?"

"Besides that," Win said, unable to stop his mouth twitching. He never quite knew when to take his uncle seriously.

"For heaven's sake, how much do decent chairs cost? You know, the Harlings have never been cheap. Frugal, yes, but not cheap."

"This from a man who hasn't bought a suit since 1970?"

"Don't need one."

"The map, Uncle Jonathan."

"Oh, yes." Placing one hand on the small of his back, he stretched, clearly a delaying tactic. He put the half-moon glasses he had hanging around his neck upon the end of his nose and peered more closely at the map.

Then he tapped a spot in southern Maine. "That's Marsh Point."

Win leaned over and took a look. "So it is."

"You can take Interstate 95 north to Kennebunkport, then get off on Route 1. There'll be signs you can follow."

"'You' as in me?"

"Of course."

"Why would I go to Marsh Point?"

Uncle Jonathan exhaled, pursing his thin lips in disgust. "Do I have to spell everything out for you, Winthrop? Hannah Marsh is there."

"I know, but what—"

"She's probably curled up by the fire with her stolen view of the ocean, studying Anne Harling's diary for clues about where she can lay her greedy little hands on the Harling Collection and our copy of the Declaration of Independence."

Win stood back and crossed his arms over his chest, trying to figure out his uncle. "I thought you liked her."

"Did I say that? I'm strictly neutral. I don't like her or dislike her. I can objectively admit she's an attractive woman who might discombobulate a stubborn monk like yourself, but that's not to say I trust her." He yanked off his smudged glasses. "She can't help being born a Marsh. It's in her genes to want whatever she can get from us."

"How do you know what she wants is the copy of the Declaration of Independence?"

"I don't. Maybe it's just you."

Win scowled.

"The point is," Uncle Jonathan went on impatiently, "you can't wait for her to make the next move."

"Uncle, Uncle," Win said, "who says I'm waiting?"

WITHIN TWO DAYS Hannah knew she would have to take another crack at the Harlings of Boston. Specifically, at J. Winthrop Harling.

Although she'd resolved to put him out of her mind, she had done a little research on him, thanks to computer modems, her local library and Cousin Thackeray's pack-rat habits. Most interesting was the article on him she'd unearthed in *The Wall Street Journal*. It painted the picture of a financial wizard even richer than Hannah had guessed. He had surprised no one by leaving New York for Boston. It was apparently his destiny to restore the Harlings' position as an active financial and social force in the community. Having a prestigious name wasn't enough for him. His purchase of the Harling House on Louisburg Square was, he was quoted as saying, only the beginning, a small step.

Cotton Harling's hanging of an innocent woman back in 1693 wasn't even mentioned. Steeped as she was in Priscilla's story, Hannah found this omission insulting. "How 'bout a little perspective?" she complained to Cousin Thackeray.

He sniffed. "Precisely what the Marshes have been saying for three hundred years. One doesn't begrudge the Harlings their successes or overly enjoy their failures, but putting them in context, it seems to me, isn't too much to ask."

All the same, the article wasn't about a seventeenth-century Harling, but a late-twentieth-century one. Hannah had to admit there was a difference.

She had also learned that J. Winthrop Harling had never been married. And when he did marry, he would—according to rampant speculation and unnamed sources—likely choose a woman who could further his dream of reclaiming his family's lost heritage. It sounded pretty calculating to Hannah, but then, Win Harling could be one formidably calculating man.

Except for their kiss. That hadn't been calculated.

Or had it?

"Thackeray," she said, "there's something I've been meaning to bring up. It's about the Harling Collection."

He groaned, throwing down his newspaper. He had the business section out, but Hannah knew he'd been reading the comics. "I thought you'd given up on that angle."

"Did you know a Marsh had been accused of stealing it?"

"Even were we all dead and gone for a hundred years, the Harlings will blame us for anything that happens to them that they don't like."

"I'm not talking about us. I'm talking about your Uncle Thackeray, the man you were named for. Not long after the Marshes moved to Maine, the Harlings accused him of having stolen a collection of valuable family papers."

"Where'd you hear this?"

"I found mention of it in an old Maine newspaper."

Her elderly cousin snatched up his paper and flipped back to the comics, not bothering to pretend he was reading about the latest stock market tumble. "So?"

"So I'm just wondering if things between the Harlings and the Marshes aren't exactly what they seem."

His eyes, as green as hers, narrowed at her over the top of his newspaper. "What have I been trying to tell you these past weeks?"

"Thackeray, did the Marshes steal the Harling Collection?"

He didn't even look up. Chuckling, he wagged a finger at her and made her read a comic strip he found particularly amusing. Hannah didn't laugh. She thought her cousin was being deliberately obtuse.

To clear her head and sort out her thoughts, she headed out to the rocks. The tide was coming in, and the wind out of the north was brisk and cold, but the sun glistened on the water. Hannah climbed down below the waterline, out of sight from Thackeray's house or her own cottage. Careful not to slip on the barnacle-covered rocks, she squatted in front of a yard-wide tide pool soon to be inundated. Waves swirled and frothed all around her. Wearing her jeans, sweatshirt and sneakers, she felt more like herself than she had in weeks.

A crunching sound on the rocks behind her startled her, and she started to fall backward, putting out a hand to brace herself. She felt barnacles slicing into her palm and cursed. It was probably just a damned sea gull. Obviously she wasn't used to being back in the country yet, away from the city of the Harlings.

"I thought for a minute there you were heading for the sharks," Win Harling said above her.

"You!"

He jumped lightly from a dry rock, landing next to her tide pool. He grinned. "Me."

Hannah regained her balance and shot to her feet, the wind whipping her hair. Caught completely off guard and seeing Win, so damned breathtaking, so incredibly sexy, so *unexpected*, she needed a few extra seconds of recovery time. "I thought you were a sea gull...."

He laughed. "I suppose people have thought worse about me. Are you all right?"

"Fine."

But he took her hand into his own and examined the scrapes from the barnacles. The skin hadn't broken. His touch was gentle, careful.

"I'll stick it in the ocean," she said, still breathless. "Ice-cold salt water's a great cure for just about anything."

"Anything?"

She saw the heat in his eyes. "Win, we need to talk...."

But talk, she knew, would have to come later. He lifted her into his arms while the wind churned the waves at their feet, spraying them with a fine, cold mist but all she could feel was the warmth of wanting him.

"I'd hoped I could think with you out of town," he murmured, "but I couldn't. All I could think about was you—and this."

She tilted up her chin until her mouth met his, their lips brushing tentatively at first, then hungrily, eagerly. His hands slipped under her Windbreaker to the warm skin at the small of her back, and she sank against his chest, trying, even on the cold, windswept rocks, to meld with his body.

Then a wave crashed into the tide pool and soaked them to their ankles, its icy water a shock to their overheated systems.

Win swore.

Hannah smiled and brushed strands of hair from her face. "Welcome to Maine."

HANNAH'S COTTAGE was about what Win had expected. Its cedar shingles weathered to a soft gray, it stood amid tall pines above the rocks. In the tiny living room, the picture window provided a view of the ocean. A fire in the stone fireplace was just dying down as they entered. Hannah pulled off her wet sneakers and socks and set them in front of the fire while she stirred the red-hot ashes. She threw on some kindling while Win, also barefoot by now, wandered down the short hall, taking note of the two small bedrooms and bath, then back up the hall and into the kitchen, all knotty pine and copper-bottomed pans. The entire floor area would probably fit into his dining room and foyer. It would be sort of like sticking a map of New England inside a map of Texas.

In contrast to the sparsity of his furnishings and the impersonal, motel-like quality of his spacious rooms on Louisburg Square, every inch of Hannah's cottage was crammed with stuff. Pot holders, hummingbird magnets, wildlife wall calendars, samplers cross-stitched with silly sayings, old quilts, throw pillows, odd bits of knitting, photo albums, pottery bowls and teapots; all of it vied for space with the mountains of books, files, notebooks, clippings and office equipment.

The only order he could sense was indirect: Hannah Marsh seemed absolutely at home here. She padded about with an ease that he hadn't sensed in Boston.

He spotted a yellowed newspaper picture of himself, then saw that it was the vile profile from *The Wall Street Journal*. He hadn't agreed with the writer's highly subjective, not to mention uncomplimentary, slant on his motives for making money. Couldn't a man simply be drawn to a job that he did well and that also happened to pay well?

The fire caught and Hannah stood back, appraising her handiwork with satisfaction. Or relief? Perhaps it had occurred to her that he might have suggested they manage without a fire.

"Nice place," Win said. "How long have you lived here?"

"Almost five years."

"Before that?"

"Oh, here and there. I traveled a lot."

She wasn't so much being evasive, he thought, as cryptic, holding back a part of herself from him. But that was all right. He had conducted his own research into the life of Hannah Priscilla Marsh, finding a thorough, if brief, biography of her in *The New York Times Book Review*'s critique of her study of Martha Washington. Hannah, the only child of an army officer and his would-be artist wife, had led the peripatetic life of a member of a military family until her father's death in a helicopter crash when she was fourteen. She and her mother had then wandered from art school to art school, until Hannah had finally gone off to college. Her mother had eventually settled in Arizona, making her living as a painter and teaching as a volunteer in low-income neighborhoods. Her death five years ago had left Hannah alone, until she'd found her cousin and Marsh Point...and that elusive sense of belonging Win thought he understood.

These details were just a few important pieces of the puzzle that was Hannah Marsh.

"How's your uncle doing?" she asked, her tone conversational.

"Just fine, thanks."

"Did he ever report his break-in to the police?"

Win thought he detected a note of suspicion in her tone. "No, why?"

"Just curious."

More than curious, he decided. "You have a theory, don't you?"

"Nope."

She shoveled free a space on the sofa for him and disappeared into the kitchen without another word. Win sighed and sat down. The fire crackled, and he could hear the rhythmic crashing of the waves on the rocks. It was an almost erotic sound. Or maybe his mind was just being driven in that direction.

Hannah, Hannah.

She wandered back in a few minutes with a tray of mugs, teapot, English butter cookies and crackers. She set them down upon an old apple crate she used as a coffee table, atop a stack of overstuffed manila folders. "Be back in a sec," she said, and disappeared again. When she returned, she held a pottery pitcher, sugar bowl and a tea strainer, which she set over one of the mugs.

She poured the tea, and he immediately noted that it was purple. Honest-to-God ordinary tea was bad enough.

She smiled. "It's black currant—very soothing."

"Do I look as if I need soothing?"

Color spread into her cheeks. Seeing her discomfort—her awareness—was almost worth having to drink purple tea. "It's great with milk and sugar," she added quickly, "almost like eating a cobbler."

The "almost" was a stretch, but at least he could drink the stuff without gagging.

"Do you like it?" she asked, seating herself on a rattan rocker.

"It tastes like tea with something that shouldn't be in tea."

"I've been drinking more herbal teas lately."

"Not sleeping well?"

Her eyes, shining and so damned green, met his, and she smiled, knowing, he guessed, what he was thinking. "You flatter yourself, Win Harling."

"I'm not keeping you awake nights?"

"Nope."

He laughed. "That's two lies—or at best half truths—so far. Want to go for a third?"

She scowled at him, sipping her tea, clearly savoring it, rather than gulping it down, as he was his, in an effort to finish the job.

Leaning forward, he said, "Tell me you're not glad to see me."

"Are you asking me?"

"Yes, I'm asking you. Are you glad to see me?"

A smile tugged at the corners of her mouth. "What'll you do if you believe I'm lying?"

"That would be three lies in a row. I don't know. I guess I'd figure something out."

"Then the answer is yes. Yes, I'm glad to see you." She set her mug upon one knee, everything about her challenging him. "Now it's for you to decide if I'm lying or not."

He took one last swallow of the purple tea and set down his mug, then leaned forward again, so that his knee touched hers, and brushed one finger across her lower lip. It was warm and moist. Her eyes were wide with desire.

"I think a part of you isn't lying," he said, "and a part is."

"Do you know which part is which?"

He could hear the catch in her voice, the breathlessness. She had pulled off her sweatshirt; underneath it she wore a long-sleeved navy T-shirt. The fabric wasn't particularly thin, but he could see the twin points of her nipples, whether still from the cold or in reaction to him, he couldn't be sure. He made no attempt to disguise his interest.

"I think I do," he said, and this time he could hear the catch, the breathlessness in his own voice. He raised his eyes to hers. "Time for one part to listen to the other, wouldn't you say?"

"Should my mind listen to my body or my body listen to my mind?"

"Decide, Hannah. Decide, because your purple tea hasn't soothed me one little bit."

He skimmed her nipples with his fingertips, inhaling deeply, wanting her more than he'd ever wanted any woman. But he knew he had to hold back. Knew he couldn't touch her again, because if he did, he would be lost. He would never get Hannah Marsh out of his system.

Her breathing was rapid now, and he could see the pulse beating in her throat. But she didn't draw closer.

"It's your decision, Hannah. It has to be."

"Why?"

"You didn't invite me here. I came. I thrust myself back into your life. It's your decision if I stay."

She licked her lips, but pulled her lower lip under her top teeth. Didn't move.

"How long do I have?" she asked.

He tried to smile. "Now, Hannah." He knew how tortured he must sound, but couldn't help it. "Decide now."

8

HANNAH JUMPED UP, spilling her tea. She raked her hands through her hair. Every millimeter of her wanted to fall to the floor with Win Harling and make love with him, until neither of them had the strength left to accuse the other of anything. Instead she said, "You need to meet Cousin Thackeray."

Win remained seated on the couch. She wasn't deceived by his outward composure. His eyes were half-closed, studying her. His mouth was set in a grim, hard line. The muscles in his arms and legs were tensed. Everything about him was taut, coiled, ready for action.

And she knew what kind of action.

She wondered if his scrutiny would ever end. She watched the tea seep into her dhurrie carpet and wondered if the purple stain would forever be a visible reminder of her encounter with a real, live Harling. A warning of the perils of her own nature. A symbol of regret, of what might have been.

She should have stuck to dead Harlings.

Finally he slapped one hand on his knee and rose with a heavy sigh. "Okay, let's go."

"You're sure it's okay?"

"Hell, no. I'd rather carry you into your bedroom and make love to you until sunup, but—"

"That's not what I meant." She felt heat spread through her. "Cousin Thackeray—are you sure you want to meet him? He doesn't care for Harlings."

"Has he ever met one?"

"He says he did decades ago, but he won't give me a straight answer."

Win nodded thoughtfully, and Hannah grabbed her squall jacket, glad to have the added cover. She could still feel the physical effects of wanting this man she had absolutely no business wanting. Even his gaze sparked pangs of desire in her. But she had to maintain control. She couldn't give in to her yearning...until she was sure she was doing the right thing.

"Well," he said, "let's go see if he decides to run me off with a shotgun."

"He doesn't own a shotgun. I'd watch out for a hot poker, though."

"A charming family, you Marshes."

They followed the narrow gravel path to the dirt road that connected Hannah's cottage to the main driveway. The wind made the air feel more like winter. Cousin Thackeray's few pitiful tulips seemed to be wishing they could close up again and come out when it was really spring. Walking beside her, Win didn't appear to notice the cold. Maybe he even welcomed it.

Thackeray's truck was still outside, but he didn't answer his door. Hannah pounded again. "Thackeray, it's me, Hannah."

No answer.

"He must have gone for a walk," she guessed. "Or maybe one of his buddies from town picked him up for a game of chess, although he usually lets me know when he's going out."

"He could be taking a nap."

"Are you kidding?" But she pushed open his back door, unlocked as always, and poked her head inside. "Thackeray?"

"We can look around out here," Win suggested, "or try again later. What have you told him about your trip to Boston?"

"Everything." She cleared her throat, feeling hot and achy with desire, and added quickly, "Except about you, of course."

He smiled. "Of course."

"It would only upset him."

"I understand."

She wondered if he did. "Does your uncle—"

"He knows to stay out of my private life. Not that it stops him."

"Does he really think I broke into his apartment and stole Anne Harling's diary?" But she didn't wait for an answer, springing ahead of Win to reach the driveway again. She cut over the side yard, heading toward the rocks. "You know, we only have your uncle's word for what happened."

"Meaning?"

"Meaning it's possible he made up the whole thing."

"You mean he pulled apart his entire apartment himself?" Win said dubiously.

Hannah knew she was on shaky ground; she could just imagine how she'd react if Win said something similar about Cousin Thackeray. "I'm not saying it's likely, just possible. I know *I* didn't do it."

He caught up with her. "What would be his motive?"

She shrugged, proceeding with caution. "Nothing devious, for sure. Cousin Thackeray would probably pitch me onto the rocks for saying this, but I actually like your uncle. I wouldn't want to believe he was up to anything truly underhanded."

"Such as?"

Inhaling, she went ahead and said it. "Getting Marsh Point back into Harling hands."

She continued walking, but Win stopped, not speaking. Up ahead, she could see Thackeray among the low-lying blueberry bushes with his binoculars, looking out at two cormorants diving for food.

"Thackeray!" she called, and waved.

He lowered his binoculars and turned, spotting her and waving back. She could see his grin.

"I've got somebody for you to meet!"

Behind her, Win said, "No."

She whipped around. "What do you mean?"

"I mean I'm not going to wait and see if I pass Thackeray Marsh's inspection. I'm not going to let you let him decide for you whether or not we—you and I, Hannah, no one else—go forward. I won't make it that easy for you." His black eyes searched hers for long seconds, and she saw in them not only physical longing, but a longing that came from his heart, maybe even his soul. "You're going to have to decide this one for yourself."

He about-faced and marched down the path toward her cottage.

Hannah gulped, not knowing what to do.

Cousin Thackeray was heading in her direction. Not fast—he never moved fast. Had she dragged Win out here to meet him, just so she could avoid making any decision about their relationship herself? What if Thackeray didn't like Win?

What if he did?

She sighed. It shouldn't matter how Thackeray felt. Win was right. "The bastard," she muttered.

But she didn't chase down the path after him. Instead she trotted across the windy point, toward the old man to whom she owed her loyalty, if not her life.

"YOU'RE SULKING."

"I'm not sulking."

Thackeray squinted at her in the bright sunlight, but didn't argue. He thrust his binoculars at her. "Look, a loon."

Hannah had no interest in his loon sighting and just pretended to focus the binoculars, while Thackeray gestured and gave instructions. "I see it," she said dispiritedly.

He hissed in disgust and yanked the binoculars away. "No, you didn't. There's no loon out there."

She pursed her lips. "That was a cheap trick."

"No matter." He gave her a long look. "Do you want to tell me about the Jaguar with Massachusetts plates parked at your cottage and that man I saw with the distinctly Harling build?"

Distinctly Harling build? What did Cousin Thackeray know? But she gave up before she even started. She was confused enough as it was.

"It's Win Harling," she told him.

"The younger J. Winthrop."

She nodded.

"Why's he here?"

"I'm not sure."

"They're after Marsh Point, aren't they, he and his uncle?"

Hannah hesitated only a moment. "It's possible. I have no proof, of course, but the uncle's story about his apartment being ransacked and Anne Harling's diary turning up missing strikes me as a bit fishy."

"Me, too. Think Win's a party to it?"

"It's hard to say. He's about as loyal to his uncle as I am to you."

Thackeray scowled and hung his binoculars around his neck. "What the devil's loyalty got to do with anything? A Marsh thinks for himself—or herself. You don't do what's wrong out of some skewed sense of loyalty. You do what's right for you."

But what if what's right for me is falling in love with J. Winthrop Harling?

"Hannah," Thackeray said when she didn't respond.

She turned to him. His nose was red in the cold air, his ratty corduroy jacket was missing a button. He was like a grandfather to her, a father, an uncle. Most of all, he was a friend. "I won't do anything that would make you hate me," she said.

"What in hell could make me hate you?" he scoffed.

She looked toward her cottage.

Then Thackeray Marsh surprised her with a hearty, warm laugh, one that reminded her he had led a long, full life. Still laughing, he headed through the blueberry bushes that were just beginning to get their foliage.

"What's so damned funny?"

"You and that Win fellow. My God, wouldn't that set three centuries of Marsh and Harling bones rattling?"

"I don't give a damn. We're talking about my life here, you know."

He stopped and spun around so abruptly that for a moment she thought he'd lose his footing. But she had never seen him so steady. "That's right," he said intently, his laughter gone. "It's *your* life."

With that, he pounded back to his house.

When Hannah returned to her cottage, Win was staring out her picture window. She controlled a rush of desire at seeing his tall, lean body, at seeing him still there.

"I thought you might have cut your losses," she said.

He looked around, the corners of his mouth twitching. "Sounds a bit drastic, don't you think?"

She refused to blush. "Witty, witty."

"I try." But his humor didn't reach his eyes, and he asked, "Do you want me to leave?"

"No. No, I don't."

"Who decided?"

"I did."

He nodded. "Good."

"I owe Cousin Thackeray a lot, and I'd never deliberately hurt or disappoint him, but not making up my own mind about things . . ." She paused, searching for the right words, the courage to be honest. "Not making up my own mind about you—that isn't what he wants from me, even if it were something I could ever give."

Win was silent.

"Do you understand?"

"Yes," he replied.

"And you believe me?"

He smiled, the humor now reaching his eyes. "This time."

"Win Harling . . ."

"Shall we go talk to the old buzzard?"

She laughed. "I believe he used the same expression to describe your uncle. I thought we . . ." She felt blood rush to her face. "Never mind. I guess it's your turn to torture me."

"Hannah, Hannah," he said in a low, deliberately sexy voice, "you haven't seen anything yet."

THACKERAY MARSH PROVED as irascible as Win had anticipated. He and Hannah joined the old man at his drafty house for lemon meringue pie that must have been around for days and coffee that tasted as if it had been poisoned. Win later learned that Hannah's cousin had reheated it from his pot that morning. A waste-not, want-not family. Hannah, he noticed, drank every drop.

"So," Thackeray said, "how's that old goat of an uncle of yours?"

"He's quite well, thank you."

Win glanced at Hannah but couldn't will her to meet his eyes. She was sitting cross-legged on a threadbare braided rug in front of a roaring fire. Southern Maine's evening temperature had plummeted; there was even talk of frost.

"We met back before the war. He was a frosty old bastard even then. Heard a Marsh had dared set foot in Boston and hunted me down, warned me one day the Harlings would get Marsh Point back. He called it Harling Point, o' course." Thackeray fastened his intense gaze—his green eyes bore a disturbing resemblance to his young relative's—on Win, who didn't flinch. "That why you're here?"

Win worded his reply carefully. "I'm not interested in pressing the Harling case for Marsh Point, no."

Thackeray grunted. "They don't have a case."

"Then why worry?"

"Who said I'm worried?"

Definitely irascible. Hannah smiled, visibly amused, as she uncoiled her legs and rested on her arms. Win wished, not for the first time, that he hadn't been so damned noble and had instead made love to her before offering to chitchat with her elderly cousin.

Before heading out, she had insisted on taking a quick shower—he hoped she'd had to make it cold—and had twisted her hair into a long French braid that hung down her back. Win still didn't know how he'd stopped himself carting her off to the bedroom there and then. Even now it amazed him.

With her hair pulled off her face, her eyes seemed even bigger, more luminous. She had changed into leggings that conformed to every shapely turn of thigh and calf and left him imagining how her legs would feel entwined with his. Her top left much more to the imagination. It was a huge sweatshirt she must have picked up in Vermont; it had a Holstein's head on the front and its behind on the back, with Enjoy Our Dairy Air in black lettering. Apparently she collected T-shirts and sweatshirts. She had shown him one of the Beatles, circa 1967. It was another side of the scholarly Hannah Marsh, as was her Hannah of the Cincinnati Harlings. A complex woman.

"Win came to Maine to make sure I hadn't made off with Anne Harling's diary," she informed her elderly cousin, "which his uncle still insists I stole."

"He only wants to know the truth," Win amended. "So do I."

Thackeray waved them both off. "I'll bet you a day's work Anne Harling didn't keep a diary any more than I did."

Hannah shook her head. "It wouldn't surprise me. Upper-class women of that era quite commonly kept diaries...."

"*She* didn't."

But Hannah didn't give in, so Win sat back and observed while the two argued about the journal-keeping habits of late-nineteenth-century women. It was a spirited discussion, given, at least to Win, the dry nature of the topic. As far as he could tell, the two Marshes didn't even disagree.

"But back to Win's Uncle Jonathan," Hannah said, and Win's interest perked up. He saw the flush of excitement in her cheeks and smiled, not just wanting her, but liking her. "He indicated Anne Harling was the one who pulled together the Harling Collection, his theory being that I stole her diary to look for clues as to the collection's location."

"That's ridiculous," Thackeray said.

"Of course. The Harlings have had the diary—if it exists—for a hundred years, and certainly would have noticed any reference to a collection that could contain a valuable copy of the Declaration of Independence."

Win couldn't let that one go unanswered. "Maybe they never read it," he speculated. "Or maybe in your research you learned something that suggested to you a passage in the diary was really a disguised clue, something we wouldn't have recognized all these years. Maybe," he went on, ignoring Thackeray's snort of disgust, "you weren't looking for the diary itself, but stole it because it was the only thing of potential value in my uncle's apartment."

Hannah fastened her cool academic's gaze on him without an inkling, he suspected, of the elemental response it produced in him. He could have hauled her off to her cottage and made love to her all night.

He might yet.

No, he thought, not might. Would.

"I suppose," she said reasonably, "there are a number of reasonable theories to fit the supposed facts. But as I said, I'll manage my biography of Priscilla Marsh without the Harling Collection."

She climbed to her feet in a lithe movement that made him think of what they were going to be like in bed together. Considering her preoccupied state, Win thought, delaying the inevitable perhaps hadn't been wise.

"Thanks for the pie, Thackeray."

The old man jerked his head toward Win but addressed Hanna. "Is he going back tonight?"

Win shook his head, answering for himself. "No."

"You're going to stay at Hannah's cottage?"

She nodded, answering for her guest.

Thackeray Marsh thought that one over. "This fellow thinks you're a thief, and you still want to put him up for the night?"

"We've called a cease-fire," Hannah said steadily. "I've paid him back for every nickel I...appropriated."

And Win had already burned her check. Its ashes were in his fireplace in Boston.

Thackeray grunted. "I'll keep my shotgun loaded by my bed. You just give a yell if you need me."

Hannah had the gall to thank him.

On their way out, Win whispered into her ear, "I thought you said he didn't have a shotgun."

She grinned. "He's full of surprises, isn't he?"

Outside it was pitch-dark, the air downright cold, the wind gusting at at least thirty miles an hour, but Hannah Marsh seemed at ease, in control, downright perky.

Win heard the gravel crunch under his feet. She seemed hardly to be hitting the ground at all. She darted ahead of him, familiar with every rock, every rut in the road to her cottage, while he stumbled along behind her.

He caught up with her. "I suggest," he said, slipping his arm around her slender waist, "you watch your yelling tonight, unless you want me blown to bits."

She turned her eyes upon him, luminous now in the starlight, and smiled softly, playfully. "Now what could possibly make me yell in the middle of the night?"

"I can think of several things."

He slipped one hand under her sweatshirt, touching the hot, smooth skin.

"Your hand's cold!"

"Serves you right."

But she didn't pull away. "Of course," she said, "I won't be the one Cousin Thackeray will shoot."

"Then the risk is all mine, isn't it?"

She shrugged, leaning against his shoulder. "I wouldn't say that."

"What's your risk?"

The gravel crunched under her feet as she came to a stop, staring at him with wide, serious eyes. "Falling for a Harling."

"Is that a bigger risk than getting shot?"

"It could be."

"Hannah . . ."

"But I'll take it," she said quickly, and darted away, into the night.

9

NOW THAT DARKNESS enveloped the cottage, Hannah felt even more alone with Win Harling . . . and surprisingly content with the situation.

He lay stretched on the floor in front of the fire, staring at the blue and orange flames. She was on her rocking chair, rummaging through tins and old cigar boxes filled with scraps of paper, clippings, coupons and recipe cards. Mostly she was trying not to think how damned appealing Win's thighs looked.

"What are you doing?" Win asked finally.

"Looking for a recipe. I've got one last pint of wild blueberries from last summer in the freezer and thought I'd make blueberry scones. Thackeray gave me the recipe—it's from his mother. They're wonderful."

"Uncle Jonathan makes blueberry scones," Win said. "He insists they're only worth making with wild blueberries. The cultivated varieties won't work."

Hannah grinned. "Cousin Thackeray says the same thing. Do you suppose those two are twins, after all?"

"Don't ever suggest that to them."

"Scandalous, isn't it? They'd probably call a truce between the Marshes and the Harlings and string us up together."

"Hannah," Win said dryly, "no hanging metaphors tonight."

She felt a rush of warmth at the way he said "tonight," as if it were just one in a long string of nights they would have together. But she didn't want to dwell on thoughts of the future and the choices it might bring, only on the present. She concentrated on the familiar smell of oak burning in the fire, the familiar sound of the gentle ebbing of the tide just beyond her cottage. Then Win moved, adding an unfamiliar sound, an unfamiliar presence as he put another log onto the fire.

"Here it is," she said, withdrawing a yellowed three-by-five index card. On it, in black ink now faded by time, Cousin Thackeray's mother had neatly printed her recipe for luscious blueberry scones.

Hannah jumped up and headed for the kitchen.

Win followed.

"You don't have to help," she told him.

"Okay." As he leaned against the sink, she noticed his narrow hips, the muscles in his thighs. "I'll watch."

She scowled. "You're in my way."

So he sat down at her small kitchen table, in front of a double window that looked onto her back porch. On the table itself stood only a wooden pepper grinder; there was neither cloth, napkins nor place mats. Hannah thought of Win's metal folding chairs and ugly dining room wallpaper and smiled, unembarrassed by her own simple existence. Never mind the fact that he could easily afford to turn the Harling House on Louisburg Square into a showpiece, that he wouldn't need a mortgage to buy Marsh Point.

He doesn't want to buy it, she thought suddenly. *He wants to prove the Marshes appropriated it from the Harlings.* . . .

She wouldn't dwell on that little problem right now.

"Are you going to just sit there and watch me?" she asked somewhat irritably.

He shrugged, obviously amused, knowing just what kind of distraction he was. "Why not?"

Why not, indeed? She tore open the refrigerator door and dug around inside until she found a bottle of beer behind smidgens of leftovers of this and that she'd promised herself would go into a pot of soup. More likely they'd end up in the garbage.

She handed Win the beer. "It's my last one."

"Don't you want it?"

"I'm not much on beer. I bought a six-pack for friends who came to visit—oh, around New Year's, I guess it was."

"Your last company?"

"Hmm? I don't know. . . ." She thought a few seconds. "No, I had friends over a couple of months ago."

"A couple of months ago," he repeated.

"I do more entertaining in the summer, and I've been so involved with my work I haven't had time for a lot of outside activities. I get out for dinner every once in a while with friends." She pulled her pint of wild blueberries from the freezer. "And I see Cousin Thackeray just about every day."

"Do you like living here in Maine?"

"Yes."

"Your cousin has no children," Win guessed.

She looked around. "Are you trying to ask me if I'm his heir? If so, yes, I am. He plans to leave me Marsh Point. Then, if you Harlings want to go toe to toe with me over who rightfully owns it, that's fine. I'll take you on. Just leave Thackeray alone."

Win didn't respond at once, but sat back in his oak chair and stretched his long legs, taking up more of her small kitchen than anyone had since she'd banished Cousin Thackeray's old Irish setter. The man simply wasn't built on the same scale as her cottage.

"So you're protecting your cousin," he said at length.

"I'm not protecting anyone. I have nothing to hide. I'm just giving you fair warning: I won't let Cousin Thackeray lose Marsh Point."

"Especially to a Harling."

"Especially."

She set to work on her scones. She got out her chipped pottery flour canister and her sugar container, of airtight plastic so the ants wouldn't get into it, the salt and baking powder. All the while she was intensely aware of Win's eyes on her. Finally she thrust the blueberries at him. "There might be a few stems and leaves floating around," she told him.

He insisted on doing a thorough job, spreading the blueberries on paper towels and examining every single one of them for stems, leaves, brown spots, bird pecks. Hannah was amused. "I usually just dump the lot into the batter and hope for the best."

"I'll keep that in mind," he said, "should I ever eat anything else I haven't supervised you cooking."

Besides the scones, supper included eggs, scrambled with fresh chives, and a carrot and raisin salad she threw together because she figured carrot sticks were too ordinary for company. Or maybe because she needed to do one more thing before sitting down kitty-corner to Win at her own kitchen table. She tasted none of the food, not even the scones. All her senses were focused on the rich, handsome, sexy rogue of a Bostonian who had come, it seemed, to dominate her very being.

"Are the scones like your uncle's?" she asked.

"Very much. It could be the same recipe."

But he was no more interested in discussing wild blueberry scones than she was. She could see it in his eyes, in the tensed muscles of his arms. He was as preoccupied with her as she with him.

It was not a comforting thought.

After dinner, they moved back into the living room, and for the first time in years, Hannah wished she owned a television set. She would have loved to turn on the news or have the idle chatter of a sitcom in the background. With just the crackle of the fire and the rhythmic washing of the ocean, it was as if there were nothing more in her world than the little cottage on Marsh Point and the man who'd come to visit.

Except that he hadn't come to visit. He had come to find out if her desire to examine the Harling Collection had prompted her to ransack his uncle's apartment and steal an old diary, so that she could later steal a rare and valuable copy of the Declaration of Independence.

He had come to find out if she was a thief.

"There are sheets in the bathroom," she said suddenly.

Win glanced at her from his spot in front of the fire. He had left plenty of room for her to join him, but she'd flopped into her rocker again, well out of reach. She could feel the warmth of the fire licking at her toes. Her fingers, however, were icy cold.

"For the bed in the guest room," she added.

"Ahh. I see."

She thought he did.

Still, she found herself trying to explain. "There's no point...your uncle...my cousin...this business about the Harling Collection and the Declaration of Independence..." She lifted her shoulders and let them fall again. "You know."

"I know," he responded. His voice was soft and liquid, filled with understanding. There was none of the hardness or defensiveness she would have expected.

Didn't he care?

She jumped up and snatched a tome on the Puritans from a pile of books next to her desk. "I'm done in. I've had a long day. I'll check the guest room and make sure everything's in order before I turn in. Do you want me to make the bed?"

"No," he said calmly, "I'll get it."

He doesn't care, she thought. She had been projecting her own desire onto him, thinking that because she wanted him that he must, therefore, want her. Which he had. Definitely. Only clearly not as much as she had him. Or at least he didn't now, which was the whole point.

I'm not making any sense.... I must be more tired than I thought.

As she flounced from the living room, she noticed he was hoisting a fat log onto the fire and arranging it with his bare hands, as if oblivious to the flames. "Don't set yourself on fire," she called over her shoulder.

"Too late," he said, half under his breath.

She slammed into the guest room. It was freezing. The curtains were billowing in the wind and the shade was flapping. Hannah quickly shut the window. When had she opened it? Not this morning. Yesterday? The day before? It had rained buckets one night.

She ran one hand over the twin bed.

Damp.

No, she thought, soaked.

She tiptoed out to the bathroom, got a couple of towels and hurried back, spread the towels on the mattress and patted them down so they could absorb as much moisture as possible. She let them sit a minute while she returned to the bathroom and grabbed sheets. If she made the bed, maybe Win wouldn't notice the wet mattress.

Her job done, she scooped up the damp towels and carted them off to her room, where her guest would be less likely to run into them. Given his suspicious mind, he'd think the worst.

"Making the man sleep in a wet bed *is* pretty bad," she admitted under her breath.

But what was the alternative?

She wouldn't think about it. The alternative, she knew, was too tempting . . . too much like what she re ally wanted. Instead she pulled on her flannel night-gown—it was a cool night, after all—and climbed into bed with her book on the Puritans. It was dry stuff. She gave up after a couple of paragraphs and picked up a mystery that lay on her night table.

About forty minutes later she was dozing between paragraphs, fighting nightmares, when footsteps in the hall startled her. Then she remembered she wasn't alone. It wasn't so much that she had forgotten Win's presence as that his footsteps were a tangible reminder of it.

"Good night, Hannah," he said softly.

"Good night. If you need anything, just give a yell."

In a few minutes he yelled, all right. *"Hannah!"*

He was back at her door in a flash, but Hannah casually dog-eared her page and yawned before she looked up. The door stood open now.

"Oh, dear," she muttered.

Send a man to lie on a cold, wet mattress, she thought, and pay the consequences.

J. Winthrop Harling was standing in her doorway in nothing but his shorts. As shorts went, they weren't much. But Hannah's attention was riveted on what they didn't cover. Long, muscular legs. A flat abdomen. A line of dark hair that disappeared into the waistband of his shorts.

He, of course, seemed totally unaware of his near-naked state.

"Is something wrong?" she asked innocently.

"The mattress is wet."

"It is?"

"Clammy, cold, wet."

"You aren't the sort of guest who would be too polite to point out something like that, I see."

His eyes seemed to clamp her against her headboard. "I'm never too polite."

"Well, I left the window open when it rained the other night. I suppose a little rain must have gotten onto your bed. I didn't notice when I made it up."

"Liar."

Succinct and accurate. She sighed. "Can't you make the best of the situation?"

"Oh, yes." He leaned against the doorjamb, suddenly looking quite relaxed, even more darkly sexy. "I can make the best of the situation."

Her heartbeat quickened. She waved her hand in the direction of the living room. "You can always camp out by the fire. I have a sleeping bag you can borrow. It's good to twenty degrees below zero."

"A good hostess," he said, "would give me her bed."

Her mouth went dry. "But I'm already in it."

As responses went, she could have done better. Win took a step into her room, her space. But just one step was enough. "Exactly."

There was no undoing, she thought, what she'd already done. She had told him he could stay. She had told him in effect that she wanted a relationship with him. A romantic relationship. A physical relationship. She had let him see a part of her she usually kept hidden. Oh, she could still send him packing. It wasn't too late. And he'd go. He'd already made it plain that he understood when no meant no.

But she didn't want him to go. She had made her choices and there had been reasons for them, even if there were also very good reasons for choosing the opposite.

She knew, with a certainty that had escaped her earlier, that she wanted him to stay.

Something in her expression must have told him so, for he took another few steps into her room. She didn't stop him.

Finally he stood next to her bed, staring down at her. "Flannel, hmm?"

"It's a year-round fabric in Maine."

"How practical."

"I bought Cousin Thackeray a nightshirt just like this one for his birthday last year. I've had this one for . . . I don't know, it must be going on four years. It's got a couple of holes." She held up one arm so he could see the burn hole in the sleeve. "The fire got me one morning."

"Hannah . . ."

"You know, don't make the mistake of thinking I'm a rube or anything. I've lived most of my life in the city. And here we're just a couple of hours from Boston. Just because I sleep in a flannel nightgown doesn't mean I'm unsophisticated. I've turned down teaching positions at Ivy League colleges."

"Hannah . . ."

"I'm sometimes torn between city and country."

"Hannah . . ."

"It's just that Marsh Point is the only real home I've ever known. My mother did the best she could after my father died, but she was chasing her own demons—and rainbows. We all do."

Finally Win just threw back the covers and climbed into bed with her. She stared at him. He grinned. "After getting into that snow cone you call a guest bed and standing here for ten minutes, I'm about to freeze."

She stuck out a toe and found his calf. "You don't feel cold to me."

"You're in the wrong place," he said, a little raggedly.

"Oh."

Even with the cold wind, Hannah had the curtainless windows in her bedroom open. Win said, "I guess I should have brought my own flannel nightshirt."

"Do you have one?"

He sighed.

"Well, they are toasty."

"I prefer," he said, "other methods of staying warm."

"Like electric blankets, I suppose. I don't believe in them, myself. I won't say they cause cancer, but they sure do waste electricity, and they're not very romantic. But I guess if you're allergic to down, or maybe if you turn down the heat in the house so low that you can justify the use of electricity..."

"Hannah."

"You had other methods of staying warm in mind?"

"Yes."

That silenced her. He looked so damned tempting and rakish beside her, a man who would stop at nothing to get what he wanted. Herself included? Did she dominate his list of wants tonight? But he was more complex than that. *They* were more complex than that.

But she didn't want to dwell on complexities now.

She moved closer, and he touched her mouth with his fingertips, just grazing her lips. "What do you want, Hannah Marsh?"

Without speaking, she caught up the hem of her nightgown and lifted it over her head, the cool night air hitting her warm skin. She tossed the nightgown onto the floor.

His black eyes were on her. She met his gaze head-on, without flushing.

"I've dreamed about this moment," she said honestly.

"So have I."

His mouth closed over hers, his hands skimming the soft flesh of her breasts, tentatively at first, then more boldly. She took a sharp breath when his thumbs found her nipples. The ache inside her was almost more than she could bear. But he didn't pause, merciless in his teasing and stroking, never letting up with either his mouth or his hands. She didn't want him to.

Still, it was a game two could play.

She reached forward blindly, a little awkwardly, but without embarrassment, until she felt him, already hot and ready, and before she could pull back or even hesitate, he thrust himself hard against her hand.

"I've never wanted anyone the way I want you," he whispered. "Never."

He drew back, just for a moment, sliding out of his shorts, then rolling back to her so that their bodies melded, so that she could feel the long length of him against her. She felt sexy, aroused.

"You're so beautiful," he whispered, before he began a deep, hungry, evocative kiss. He trailed his fingertips down her spine, captured her buttocks in his palms, then skimmed the curve of her hips until he found the hot, moist, ready center of her.

"Win . . . I . . ."

"It's okay," he whispered, "it's okay."

And it was. More than okay.

"I don't know if I can last. . . ."

"That's two of us."

But he hadn't finished.

"You're not going to have mercy on me, are you?" she said playfully, already knowing he wouldn't.

She let him roll her onto her back. He moved on top, his torso raised while his eyes seemed to absorb every inch of her. She splayed her fingers in the hairs on his chest, feeling the lean muscle, then let them trail lower, until they closed around his maleness. He thrust against her with a rhythm that was as primitive as the crashing of the waves upon the rocks outside her window.

His mouth descended to hers, tasted, then moved down her throat, tasted some more, and to her breasts, tasting and nipping. She wouldn't release him. Then he moved down her abdomen, tasting and licking now, not stopping.

"Let yourself go," he whispered. "Just let go."

As if she could stop herself.

But then she realized she'd never felt anything so erotic, so achingly pleasurable as his caresses.

He drew away from her, only for a moment to take precaution, before coming inside her, hard and fast, murmuring his encouragement, his love, until her cries mixed with those of the cormorants and the sea gulls and finally his body quaked with hers, rocking, shattering.

Afterward, in the stillness, she noticed the wind had died down, too, and the waves were making a gentle swishing sound, as if they had all the time in the world to get wherever they were going. Hannah listened to the ocean for a long time and smiled at the man beside her.

A Harling. In her bed.

"Do you suppose," she said, "three centuries of Harlings and Marshes are already planning ways to haunt us tonight?"

He grinned back at her. "If they are, we'll be ready for 'em, don't you think?"

After making love with him, Hannah figured she was ready for anything.

IN THE MORNING the only sign he'd been there was the blazing fire in the living room.

She was ordinarily not a heavy sleeper, so Hannah assumed that either their lovemaking at dawn had knocked her out or that Win had sneaked out on her very, very quietly. She made herself a pot of coffee, added another log to the fire, and told herself she didn't regret last night. If she had to do it over again, she would. The giving and taking, emotionally and physically, had been mutual, real, if also fleeting. She had decided last night to let tomorrow bring what it would.

And it had, hadn't it?

She called him a host of names, dumped the trash and changed her sheets, wanting a fresh start.

The name-calling didn't work. She kept seeing his dark eyes on her, hearing his deep laughter, feeling the strength and warmth of his arms around her. She kept remembering the things they had told each other in the night, about growing up and climbing trees and finding a rare piece of glassware at a yard sale for two dollars and not being able to take it, having to tell the new widow who was selling off her stuff to pay her property taxes with what it was worth. Mostly they had talked about little things. There had been nothing about Thackeray Marsh or old Jonathan Harling, nothing about the Harling Collection, the ransacked apartment, the missing diary or the Declaration of Independence.

"Oh, Hannah," Win had said, stroking her hips, the inside of her thighs. "There's never been anyone remotely like you in my life . . . never."

She remembered how she'd responded. Hotly, eagerly, more boldly than on the occasion of their first lovemaking, she had shown him where to touch her, let him show her where to touch him. They had made love with abandon. Without thought. Without inhibition.

Without commitment?

"Hannah, Hannah . . . I'll never stop wanting you," he'd added.

He had been inside her then, thrusting hard yet lovingly, and she'd had her hands on his hips, urging him on, thinking that her ache for him would never end, never be satiated, that he'd collapse first. But he hadn't. He'd murmured his encouragement, urged her to let go . . . and she'd felt his satisfaction when she'd exploded, rocked and moaned as he kept going. . . .

Now, in the bright, cold light of morning, Win Harling was gone. Calling him names wouldn't bring him back or make her hate him.

Or regret a single second of what they'd done last night. It had been a deliberate, conscious, mature choice on her part. She'd known the potential consequences.

Just as she knew that, come what may, there would never be another man for her. Win Harling was it. She wasn't the sort of woman who jumped into bed with one man one night and just hoped for the best. She had gone to bed with him because she had wanted him and only him.

Now she had to pay the price.

"Damn," she swore under her breath. She grabbed a sweatshirt, anxious for the solace of the sea, the rocks, the tide . . . for the solace of Marsh Point itself.

Outside in the chilly air, the dew soaked into her sneakers and she saw that his Jaguar was gone, too. It wasn't as if he'd ducked out for an early walk and planned to be back soon.

She didn't know if he planned to be back at all.

"The scoundrel," she muttered.

But what had she expected? She'd seen the two sides of Win Harling: the black-eyed rogue who'd chased her down in Boston and the sophisticated gentleman who hadn't pressed himself upon her yesterday, despite his plain sexual need. Had the rogue made love to her last night? The gentleman? Or some combination of the two?

"What does it matter? He's gone now."

She began her litany of names again, but none of them made her feel the slightest bit better.

10

AT SOME GREASY-SPOON diner not more than two miles from Marsh Point, Win and his uncle Jonathan sat over weak coffee and runny eggs. "You need to let me sort out this mess on my own," Win said in an attempt to reason with the old man.

Uncle Jonathan shook his head, soaking up a pool of egg with a triangle of pale white toast. "It's not your mess."

"Look . . ."

"I'm here, Winthrop. Make the best of it."

It was pointless to argue and Win knew it. Shortly after crawling out of Hannah's bed that morning and building a fire, he had slipped out to refill the wood box. He had planned to spend the morning with her, going over all the details of her trip to Boston, her research into Priscilla Marsh and Cotton Harling, her discovery of the possible existence of the Harling Collection. Everything. In turn, he'd tell her what little he'd learned from Uncle Jonathan.

Instead, out in the woodpile, he'd caught his uncle prowling about Marsh Point. Why the crazy old coot hadn't fallen and broken his hip in a tide pool was beyond him. Now there was nothing to be done but gather his things and cart Uncle Jonathan off to town, before one of the Marshes awakened and called the police.

So far, his uncle had yet to satisfactorily explain what he was doing in Maine. He had, he'd said, taken a bus from Boston and then a cab out to Marsh Point that had cost him double, he insisted, what it should have. He'd spent the night in a "disreputable" motel and had risen early and sneaked onto "the disputed property," where Win had found him.

"Has your apartment been broken into again?" Win asked.

"Nope."

"Did you find the Anne Harling diary under a couch cushion or something?"

"Nope."

"Uncle . . ."

"That cottage where I found you," Jonathan said, pouring still another little plastic vial of half-and-half into his coffee. "Hannah Marsh's, isn't it?"

Win sighed. "Yes, it is."

"She and you . . . slept together, did you?"

"Uncle Jonathan, you know I don't discuss my private life."

The old man grunted. "I'll wager you did more than sleep. My word, Winthrop. Falling for a Marsh." He let out a long breath. "No wonder I had trouble sleeping last night."

"You had trouble sleeping," Win muttered, controlling his growing frustration with difficulty, "because you know damned well you should have been home in your own bed. Uncle Jonathan, there's nothing you can do here except cause trouble. Go home."

The old man slurped his coffee and said, without looking at his nephew, "I wasn't the one who slept with a Marsh last night."

Win was at the end of his rope. "Cotton Harling and Priscilla Marsh lived three hundred years ago. I won't let them dictate to me what I should do with my life. And I don't give a damn whether we have a legitimate claim to Marsh Point or not. I don't even give a damn if Hannah would lie to her grandmother to get her hot little hands on the Harling Collection! You," he said, knowing he was losing control, "are going back to Boston."

Looking remarkably unperturbed by his nephew's outburst, Uncle Jonathan flagged the waitress for more coffee. She was back in a jiffy. Win let her heat his up. It was dreadful stuff. Almost worse than Hannah's purple tea.

Hannah, Hannah.

He had to keep Uncle Jonathan away from Thackeray Marsh and Marsh Point, at least until he and Hannah had adequately compared notes.

His uncle began again. "I talked to a friend of mine from Harvard who deals in rare books and documents."

Continually amazed by the variety of people Jonathan Harling knew, Win indulged him. "About what?"

"The copy of the Declaration of Independence in the Harling Collection."

"Allegedly."

Jonathan waved off Win's correction. "It's worth even more than I had anticipated."

"You'd anticipated a lot. How much more?"

"If it's in mint condition..."

"And if it exists."

Uncle Jonathan sighed. "It would be worth seven figures."

"Seven—"

"A million dollars."

At that moment, with Win gritting his teeth at the figure his uncle had just named, Thackeray Marsh wandered into the diner.

Directly behind him, spotting the two Harlings at once, was his cousin, the blond and beautiful Hannah Marsh.

HANNAH GLARED AT WIN and his uncle, while Cousin Thackeray gave a victorious sniff. The two Harlings looked remarkably guilty. Still, Hannah felt a rush of excitement at seeing Win, though she had to fight back memories of last night. At the same time, she didn't regret one nasty name she'd called him.

"Thackeray Marsh," Jonathan Harling declared, eyeing his contemporary with exaggerated disdain. "So you're still alive. I'd heard you were killed in the Normandy invasion. Nothing heroic, of course. Drowned stepping over your own feet."

Win scowled at his uncle who, Hannah was sure, had heard no such thing.

It was equally clear that Thackeray wasn't in the mood to help matters. "At least I fought in the war, instead of using privilege to get me a safe stateside job."

Jonathan Harling reddened and nearly came out of his chair, but Win clamped a hand on the old man's arm and held him down.

"Thackeray!" Hannah admonished her cousin.

He gave her a smug look for her trouble.

The diner was filling up with fishermen, in from their morning rounds. *All we need now is to start a brawl*, Hannah thought. "You two keep on like this," she told the two old men, "and you'll get us all arrested."

"Just stating the facts," Cousin Thackeray said loftily.

Jonathan Harling grunted. "A Marsh wouldn't know a fact if it smacked him in the face."

"Perhaps," Hannah said through clenched teeth, "we should go back to Marsh Point and discuss things."

Cousin Thackeray shook his head. "I don't want them on my property."

"*Your* property," Jonathan sneered. "Why, back in 1891—"

Win cut him off, his eyes pinned on Hannah. "How did you find us?" he asked quietly.

Before she could answer, Thackeray said, "That damned ostentatious car you drive sticks out around here like—"

Now it was Hannah's turn to do some cutting off. "My cousin found evidence of a prowler while on his morning walk and insisted it had to be a Harling. I indulged him in a spin around town, the result of which is our presence here."

"What evidence?" Jonathan demanded.

Thackeray gave him a supercilious look. "Nothing *you* would notice. I, however, who was raised out here, wondered if an elephant hadn't been through."

Win was on his feet, laying bills upon the table. His jaw was set, hard. He moved with tensed, highly controlled motions. An unhappy man. Obviously hadn't got enough sleep last night. Hannah watched him, pleased with herself. At least she wasn't the only one suffering.

"Let's go," he said, taking in both Marshes and his uncle.

"Oh, no, you don't," Cousin Thackeray replied, shaking his head. "I'm not letting you two sneak off before I get a chance to search your car and your persons."

"Fine." Win's tone was steely, but had no apparent effect on anyone. "You and my uncle can drive together. I'll take Hannah."

The two old men argued all the way out to the parking lot, but Win was adamant. He opened the passenger door to Thackeray's 1967 GMC Truck and told his uncle it was his choice: he could be helped in or thrown in. Jonathan squared his shoulders and climbed in without anyone's help. Thackeray muttered something about wanting to ram the passenger side of his truck into a tree, except for the fact that it had another five or ten years left in it, might even outlast him. Win just looked at Hannah in despair.

"We'll follow you," he told his uncle and her cousin. "No tricks."

He turned away before either could say any more.

Hannah had opened the passenger door to his Jaguar. "Any orders for me?" she asked coolly.

He glared at her. "Just get in."

She did so, slamming the door shut. He followed. His tall, lean body filled the interior, instantly making her aware again of last night, of her unceasing attraction to this man. She tried not to show it.

"I take it," she said as he started the car, "that you found your uncle snooping around this morning and sneaked out."

A muscle worked in his jaw. "That's about it."

"You made your choice, didn't you?"

"The way I see it," he said tightly, rolling into position behind Thackeray's truck, "I didn't have a choice."

"I'm not saying you shouldn't have gone with your uncle. All I'm saying is, a note or a quick goodbye would have been . . . courteous."

"And what would you have done?"

"If I knew your uncle was snooping around Marsh Point? I don't know."

"You'd have raised hell, Hannah. At the very least you'd have hauled your cousin over, and he'd have called the police and had Uncle Jonathan arrested as a trespasser." He glanced at her. "Like me, you would have felt you had no choice."

He was crowding Cousin Thackeray on the winding, narrow road out to Marsh Point. Thackeray braked hard and Win cursed, just missing the truck's rear end. But he backed off. Hannah could almost hear her cousin's satisfied chuckle.

She sighed. "I don't know if you're right or you're wrong, and I guess we'll never find out. Did your uncle tell you why he's here?"

"We were just getting into it when you and Thackeray barged in. Nice timing." He exhaled, running one hand through his wild hair. His day obviously hadn't started out very well. Neither, however, had hers. "Hannah, I'm doing the best I can. Will you believe that much?"

She didn't answer right away. They had just rounded a bend, and she could see white-capped waves pounding the rocks of Marsh Point. The sun was shining. The temperature had begun to climb. It would be a splendid day in southern Maine. But her life here, Hannah thought, would never again be the same.

Finally she said, "I'll believe that much, yes."

In a few moments, he turned into Thackeray's driveway and followed the truck up to the house. Jonathan Harling seemed to jump out before the truck had even come to a full stop. He was waving his arms and shouting.

"This should be interesting," Win said grimly.

"Think I should keep a bucket of cold water handy, in case things get out of control?"

He looked at her and grinned. "A woman after my own heart." He nodded toward the house. "Shall we?"

"As I see it," she said, paraphrasing his earlier words, "we have no choice."

HANNAH, Thackeray Marsh and Uncle Jonathan were arguing a point of early American history that held no interest for Win, but at least, he thought, no one had yet come to blows. He noticed that Hannah held her own in the argument with the two men, whom she accused of agreeing with each other, even if they wouldn't admit it. Being no historian, Win couldn't comment.

Finally he rose, feeling it was relatively safe to leave them alone, and wandered from the living room to the dining room, preoccupied not with Puritans but with a document potentially worth a million dollars. If it existed. If it could be located.

Uncle Jonathan could use the money.

So could the Marshes.

Win exhaled, walking through the French doors onto a deck that overlooked a small cove he hadn't noticed yesterday. Here the land sloped gently to the water, where waves lapped over sand and marsh grass. He squinted against the sunlight.

Something had been shoved into the brush. It was dark blue; he could see just one end.

A canoe. A wooden canoe.

His uncle was capable of many things, but not of paddling from Boston or even Kennebunkport in a canoe. He had said he'd taken a bus and a taxi, and Win believed him. Maybe it was Thackeray Marsh's canoe. Or Hannah's.

But he didn't believe it. A dark suspicion started to formulate itself in his mind.

Returning to the living room, he grabbed his uncle. "Let's go for a walk."

Uncle Jonathan was red-faced with arguing. "These two"—he jerked his head at the Marshes—"know nothing about American judicial history."

"I'm sure they don't." Win didn't give a damn if they did. "Let's go."

"Hold your horses, there. I won't have you humoring me just because I'm an old man."

"Uncle Jonathan, we need to talk. I have a proposition I want to discuss with you before I present it to Hannah and Thackeray."

It was never easy for Jonathan Harling to abandon an argument, but he took the hint and followed his nephew outside. They left behind Hannah and Thackeray, grumbling and looking very suspicious, as well they might.

"What the devil have you got a bee in your bonnet about?" Uncle Jonathan demanded. "I was being civil to those two."

"I think I know who ransacked your apartment."

The old man narrowed his eyes, then nodded solemnly. "I was wondering when you'd figure it out."

"WHAT DO YOU SUPPOSE they're up to?" Thackeray asked.

Hannah sat cross-legged on the threadbare carpet, already contemplating just that question herself. "I don't know. But don't you get the feeling they're holding more cards in their deck than we are? And don't tell me it's the Harling way."

"Well, it is."

"Win's on to something." She climbed to her feet, feeling oddly confident. Not outmatched. Not outwitted. Not as if Win Harling and his cantankerous uncle were actual enemies. Not allies, perhaps, but definitely not enemies. "I think I'll take a walk, too."

"Don't let 'em catch you."

But he sounded distracted, preoccupied with something besides his natural inclination to doubt everything the Harlings said or did. His eyes weren't focused on her. She said goodbye, but he didn't answer, didn't even wave a hand.

Something was definitely up. Was she the only one who didn't know what?

Outside the air was still and so clear that everything seemed overfocused, outlined in sharp detail against a sky so blue that it made a body appreciate life. Hannah went through the side door, just as Win and her uncle had, but saw no sign of them. She had no idea where they'd gone. Had they wandered toward her cottage? She didn't want to eavesdrop, but her trust level wasn't what it had been only a few hours ago. She wanted to keep an eye on the two Harlings.

It was ridiculous, she thought, a Marsh like herself falling for a Harling, but there it was. And she wasn't falling, she knew that much. She'd already fallen.

She was in love with the man.

They weren't anywhere outside or inside her cottage. Hannah stared out the picture window in her living room, tapping her foot and cursing them. She forced herself to return to Thackeray's house, duly noting along the way that Win's car was still parked behind her cousin's old truck. Wherever they'd gone, it couldn't be far.

She headed back inside, determined to get some straight answers out of Thackeray Marsh about the Harling claim on Marsh Point and about the missing Harling Collection.

She would not let him or Jonathan Harling sidetrack her with their inflammatory comments on some obscure historical fact. She wanted answers.

When she had them, then she would figure out what to do about Win Harling.

And find out what he meant to do about her.

Cousin Thackeray wasn't in the living room. She checked the kitchen, but he wasn't there, either. She was getting really irritated now.

"Thackeray?"

Silence.

Had he gone for a walk, too? Let them all go off, she thought. She'd be damned happy, living all alone on Marsh Point! Who needed two old men and one know-it-all, black-eyed rogue?

She groaned. How the hell could she have fallen in love with J. Winthrop Harling? He made too much money. He'd had his life handed to him on a silver platter. He probably didn't know anything about the Deerfield Massacre or the influence of covenant theology on American democracy.

"Thackeray! Dammit, where are you?"

She flounced upstairs to check the bathroom; surely he must have heard her, for all the racket she was making?

The attic door was ajar.

Creaking it open, Hannah stuck her head inside and squinted up the dark, steep staircase. She could smell the dust and mold. "Thackeray, are you up there?" she called, lowering her voice for no particular reason.

When there was no answer, she reached along the wall for a light switch, but found none. She didn't relish walking up there in the dark. But if Cousin Thackeray was up there, surely he had a flashlight and was just off in some corner? And even if he didn't, even if he wasn't up there, what else—who else—could be?

Bats, she thought. Spiders, cobwebs, mice.

"Coward," she muttered to herself and headed up.

The steps creaked and the musty odor worsened as she climbed the steep staircase. She had never been up to the attic. It was unfinished, there was no rail or wall built up around the stairwell; as her eyes adjusted to the darkness, she could see silhouettes of boxes and old furniture, but no beam of a flashlight. She was probably on a wild-goose chase, while Win and Jonathan and her cousin were all doing the real business of the day elsewhere.

"Thackeray," she called irritably, "are you up here?"

A shuffling noise came from the far corner off to her right, then a strangled cry. Her cousin's voice croaked, "Run, Hannah!"

"*Thackeray!*"

She lurched up the last three steps. The silhouette of a man emerged from behind a huge armoire. It wasn't her tall, thin, elderly cousin. Hannah quickly grabbed whatever was at her feet—a soggy box of hats, it turned out—and heaved it at the figure. It went wide. She scrambled for a stack of old drapes and started heaving them, too, but in a moment the strange figure had her, one arm clamped firmly around her middle. She kicked. He cursed viciously.

"What have you done with Thackeray?" she yelled. "Who are you? *Help!*"

But with one last, violent curse, he threw her against the armoire. She hit it hard with her right shoulder and spun into the darkness, out of control, breaking her fall with her left arm and landing unceremoniously in a heap in the pile of drapes. Her entire body ached. She let loose a string of curses herself.

"Thackeray, for God's sake, get away!"

She flung drapes at the figure behind her and leaped over the open stairwell to the other side of the attic, away from her cousin. Her pursuer followed. She could hear him breathing hard. She grabbed a ladder-back chair and shoved it into his path, knocking him off his feet.

Thackeray Marsh slipped down the stairs.

The man swore, scrambled to his feet and came after her again. "Bitch!"

There was a small, dirty window at the far end of the attic that Hannah was eyeballing for size. Would she fit? Could she make it through before her attacker caught up with her?

What happened if she did?

What happened if she didn't?

She dodged behind a metal clothes closet and dived for the window, tripping over a rolled-up rug. Adrenaline kept her from feeling any pain, any fatigue. She refused to panic. She got back to her feet.

Something to break the window... She needed something hard and within reach.

An old cane. Perfect!

Iron fingers closed around her left ankle and pulled her off her feet, sending her headlong. A heavy body landed on top of her. She felt the air going out of her lungs. Her right arm was twisted around to the small of her back, under him.

"Don't move, don't talk. I wouldn't want to hurt you."

She nodded her understanding.

And recognized his voice. The pieces of the puzzle fell together.

Her captor was Preston Fowler, director of the New England Athenaeum, to whom she had confided so much. He took a deep breath, then laughed roughly. "I might want to do other things to you," he said, stroking her hair with his free hand, "but not hurt you."

She kicked his shin as sharply as she could.

He bore down upon her twisted arm, and it was all she could do not to cry out. "You just bought yourself some pain, Miss Marsh."

"What do you want with me?"

"Don't talk."

"Tell me!"

He brought his mouth close to her ear, and she felt his breath against her cheek. "You're my ticket to a million dollars."

"I don't—"

"Shut up." He settled himself more firmly on top of her, sliding his free hand down her upper arm and just skimming her breast. "Just be quiet and still and nothing will happen to you."

She didn't move, didn't even breathe.

"You see," he said, "you're my hostage."

"WHERE THE DEVIL do you suppose he is?" Jonathan Harling asked.

Win regarded him with growing exasperation, though the feeling was directed not so much toward his uncle as the situation. They had combed the point for any sign of Preston Fowler, but found only the canoe and a single footprint in the mud. Both, they decided, had to be his. It was too early for tourists, and they had no doubt that Preston Fowler very much wanted first crack at the Harling Collection and the Declaration of Independence.

Win and his uncle headed back onto the deck of Thackeray's dining room, figuring to tell the Marshe everything.

"I don't know where he is, but if—"

Thackeray Marsh burst around the corner of th house, his thin hair sticking up, his face ashen. Hi clothes were covered with dust, and a cobweb dangle off one arm. He could hardly speak. "Hannah . . . th bastard's got her . . . he . . ."

A cold current shot through Win.

"Calm down, man," Uncle Jonathan ordered impa tiently. "We can't understand what in blazes you' saying."

Win had understood. "Where?"

Thackeray pointed to the house. "The attic . . ."

It was all Win needed to hear.

Behind him, Uncle Jonathan hissed in annoyance. "Now don't go barging in up there before you get all the facts!" He pounded his cane on the ground. "Winthrop—Winthrop, we need a plan!"

But Win was already through the French doors. He grabbed the poker from the living room fireplace and headed upstairs, the cold current now a hot rage.

Fowler. If the stinking bastard even touched Hannah . . .

He ripped open the door and took the stairs two at a time, ignoring the darkness. He thought only fleetingly about how Fowler might be armed, what he had planned. His main concern was Hannah.

Hannah . . .

At the top of the stairs he stopped and listened, let his eyes adjust to the lack of light. He heard nothing, could make out nothing that resembled Hannah or Fowler. Had the bastard already sneaked off with her?

To his left he heard a soft moan.

"Hannah?"

Holding his poker high, he moved toward the sound. He had to fight his way through scattered drapes and past overturned furniture, but remained alert. The sun was angling in through the dirty window now, casting faint light upon a figure that lay sprawled on what appeared to be a rolled-up carpet.

It moved, and the sun hit strands of long, silken, blond hair.

"Hannah," Win breathed.

Within seconds he was kneeling beside her, pulling a nasty-looking gag from her mouth, fumbling at the drapery cord that was tied around her wrists. Her eyes were huge and frightened, and damned beautiful.

She spat dust and cobwebs from her mouth, coughing, and finally sputtered, "It's a trap."

No sooner were the words out than Win felt something cold and metallic against his lower jaw. "Now have two hostages," Preston Fowler said.

"Now," Win said tightly, "you have one hell of a mess on your hands. Let us both go, before you get yoursel in any deeper."

"You arrogant, insufferable prig." Fowler laughe nastily, never moving the gun. "God, I've wanted to sa those words to one of you for years. No, do not move I warn you. As you have so accurately pointed out—a if I needed you to tell me—I'm in one hell of a mess. intend, however, to emerge from it intact."

"He thinks Cousin Thackeray has the Harling Co lection," Hannah told Win hoarsely. "He wants t Declaration of Independence. He's the one—" She ha to pause to cough, so merciless had Fowler been in a plying the gag. "He broke into your uncle's apa ment."

"I know," Win responded gently. "I should ha known from the beginning. He knew what you we working on. With your blond hair and reputation a biographer, he probably figured out you were Hann Marsh—Priscilla's descendant—right from the star

Fowler smirked. "It was a simple matter to blow her cover story straight to hell."

"So he watched you, and knowing you were an expert researcher, he followed your leads to the Harling Collection. . . ." Hannah shut her eyes, and Win could see pain and regret wash over her; it could be no worse than what he felt. He would give anything to see her smile. "Hannah, Uncle Jonathan knew it had to be Fowler who ransacked his apartment. Other than you, he was the only one who could have known about the diary or the Harling Collection."

"Oh, stop, both of you," Fowler ordered. "Let's get this over with. The Harling Collection, Miss Hannah. Where is it?"

She shook her head, not, Win could see, for the first time, and said wearily, "I told you, I don't know."

Keeping the gun pressed to Win's jaw, Fowler leaned over him and said to Hannah, "Suppose I start blowing holes in your lover boy here? Do you think that would improve your memory?"

Win made himself chuckle. "You've got that one wrong, Fowler. Give her the gun. She'll blow holes in me herself."

"Shut up!"

Win thought he heard a small, creaking sound on the attic stairs. Footsteps? Old men's footsteps?

Dear God, he thought.

He looked at Hannah and saw her eyes widen slightly. Had she heard the creaking sound, too?

Uncle Jonathan and Cousin Thackeray coming to rescue them.

It was almost more than Win could bear.

His fingers closed around the poker. One small opening was all he needed. He longed to knock Preston Fowler onto his greedy ass. But he had to cover for the two down on the staircase. Hannah, he noticed, was noisily shifting around.

"Can I untie her wrists?" Win asked.

"No, leave them. She's a vicious bitch, you know. Practically emasculated me. I'm sure you're disappointed she didn't succeed. But I won't be diverted from my task. The Harling Collection, Miss Marsh."

Behind them, Jonathan Harling's voice broke through the darkness. "It isn't hers to give away."

Then Thackeray Marsh said, "Drop the gun, Mr Fowler. I have a loaded Colt .45 pointed at your lower spine and would be glad to pull the trigger to repay you for the thrashing you gave me alone."

"You're bluffing," Fowler sneered.

"So call my bluff. Find out what happens."

"He's a mean shot," Uncle Jonathan said. "He taught me how to shoot when we were at Harvard together in the thirties. I remember he could hit a weasel from fifty yards, right between the eyes—"

"I can blow your nephew's head off," Fowler interjected.

Thackeray sniffed. "Go ahead. He's a Harling. I'll get a bullet into you before you get to Hannah."

Win's eyes locked with Hannah's. He could see she realized her cousin was having a hell of a time.

"Drop the gun," Thackeray Marsh drawled. "Slowly."

He seemed to be taking his lines from old Clint Eastwood movies, but Fowler, biting back what sounded like a curse, removed the gun from Win's jaw and slowly lowered it to the floor.

"Bastards," he muttered, "all of you."

Then he whipped around, roaring like a madman, catching everyone by surprise; he shoved the two old men aside and leaped for the stairs.

"Shoot him!" Uncle Jonathan yelled. "Shoot the greedy bastard!"

"I can't bloody see him! I'm not twenty anymore, you know, you old snot. Why the hell don't you go after him?"

"I'm eighty years old!"

"So? I'm seventy-nine."

"Take care of Hannah," Win growled. "*I'll* go after him. Mind if I borrow your gun, Thackeray?"

"Not at all, but you'd better take care. It's not loaded."

Win forced himself to refrain from comment.

"If you hadn't gone off like a decapitated chicken," Uncle Jonathan put in, "we'd have been able to take time to load the gun. As it was, Thackeray couldn't remember where he'd put the bullets. In fact, he'd almost forgotten he even had the gun. I had to remind him...."

"The hell with it," Win muttered and dashed off with
the poker. Maybe Fowler hadn't loaded his gun, ei
ther.

He fought his way through the scattered drapes and
overturned furniture, choking on cobwebs and dust
warning himself not to let his anger lead him into ar
other trap. With a near-physical effort, he dismissed th
image of Hannah bound and gagged. It must have bee
a devastating experience for her. And it was all his faul
Would she ever be the same? Would she ever forgiv
him for not having shared his suspicions sooner?

No. You'll have to deal with that later.

Fowler had shut the attic door. Win pushed again
it, but it wouldn't give. The bastard must have blocke
it. He reared back and threw all his weight at the o
door. It bounced and cracked a little, but still did
give.

"Here," Hannah said, suddenly beside him, as pa
as a ghost, "let me help."

Win saw the raw, bloody wrists, the spreading bru
on her jaw, and felt rage boil up inside him, threate
ing once again to overwhelm him.

Then he saw the gun in her hand.

"What's that?" he asked.

She smiled a little. "Fowler's gun."

Win grinned, suddenly reenergized. He pointe
thumb at the door and smiled at Hannah. "Shall w

She set the gun upon a step, and Win turned it s
wasn't pointed at either of them. He was taking no m
chances.

Uncle Jonathan and Cousin Thackeray appeared at the top of the stairs. "Heave-ho!" they yelled.

It took Hannah and Win three tries, and the door splintered into three parts before the chair Fowler had anchored under the knob gave way.

They were out.

_____ **11** _____

HANNAH IGNORED THE PAIN in her wrists and shoulders, her dry mouth, her fear. She concentrated only on keeping up with Win and trying not to shoot him or herself in the foot. Guns were not her thing.

They caught up with Fowler in Cousin Thackeray's truck. He must have snatched the keys from the hook by the back door; he was still fumbling with them when Win hauled him out of the cab and threw him onto the ground. Hannah controlled a wild impulse to fire the gun into the air.

"All right, all right!" Fowler yelled when Win twisted his arms behind his back. "I give up. Call the damned police."

Breathing hard, Win didn't let up. "You won't try anything?"

"Like what, running? You lunatics would shoot me like a dog." He spat a mouthful of grass and dirt. "Just let me go. I'll take what's coming to me."

"You're damned right you will."

Fowler glanced at Win, who still held his prisoner's arms pinned behind him. "I wouldn't have hurt anyone."

Hannah could see Win gritting his teeth. "You did hurt someone."

"She's a Marsh. One wouldn't think a Harling would go all soft over—"

He shut up when Hannah stepped forward, holding his gun. "One wouldn't think," she said, "a snooty Harling could knock you on your behind, either, but look at you now, Mr. Fowler."

"It's *Doctor* Fowler," he said loftily.

Win made a sound of pure disgust and let up, climbing to his feet. He looked at Hannah. "I'll call the police. You can keep an eye on him?"

"Sure. With pleasure."

Fowler sat up, his face red with anger, devoid of remorse. That was as far as Hannah would let him go. After her ordeal in the attic, she was taking no chances. But just as Win started for the house, they heard the wail of a siren, and Cousin Thackeray and Uncle Jonathan raced out of the back door, armed to the teeth with kitchen knives and skillets. They looked as if they were having the time of their lives.

"I've called the police," Thackeray announced.

"They're on their way," Jonathan added excitedly.

Fowler looked at his four captors and muttered, "Thank God."

The police came, explanations were made, and Preston Fowler was carted off. Charges were filed and the sorting-out process was begun. Through it all, Hannah noticed that Cousin Thackeray never once allowed that the Harlings and the director of the New England Athenaeum might be correct in their opinion that he knew the location of the long-missing Harling Collection.

She also noted that Win Harling never left her side.

The police seemed to be having a difficult time fathoming why a director of a prestigious institution like the New England Athenaeum would risk arrest to snatch a collection of old papers, even one that might include a valuable copy of the Declaration of Independence.

"How valuable?" the lieutenant in charge asked the group of people assembled in his small office.

The Marshes didn't answer. The Harlings, however, said, "A million dollars, give or take ten thousand or so."

The lieutenant, a rail-thin Maine native, whistled. "But there's no proof this thing exists?"

"None whatsoever," Thackeray Marsh replied, although the question wasn't directed at him.

Win smiled at Hannah, but said nothing. Then his gaze fell upon her bruised and raw wrists and his smile vanished, his expression darkening. The police had asked her if she needed medical attention, but she'd said no, largely because she didn't want to miss the Harlings' explanation of the day's festivities.

"And this Fowler character," the lieutenant went on, "learned about the collection—and presumably the Declaration of Independence—when Miss Marsh here was conducting research in Boston?"

"They weren't in cahoots," Thackeray put in.

"That's not what I was implying. I'm merely trying to establish the sequence of events. Miss Marsh, we'll need a statement from you on your trip to Boston and your association with Dr. Fowler."

"Certainly. I had no idea he would go to such extremes for personal profit. I myself had only an academic interest in the collection."

An eyebrow went up and the lieutenant asked, "Even though the subject of your new biography is one of your ancestors, who was wrongly executed by an ancestor of the Harlings?"

She smiled coolly. "Even so."

Jonathan Harling gave a small grunt that she managed to ignore.

Beside her, Win said, "Fowler broke into my uncle's apartment in an attempt to discover any materials that would provide him with a clue as to the location of the Harling Collection. He stole a diary written by—"

Win's elderly uncle cleared his throat and squirmed in his rickety wooden chair. "That's not quite the case. Fowler did break into my apartment, of course, and combed the place, but he didn't steal the diary. He just read it."

"He read it," the lieutenant repeated dubiously.

"That's right. It describes how the Marshes hoodwinked us out of our land here in southern Maine and stole the Harling Collection."

Thackeray was on his feet now. "It was never your land! The Marshes are the legitimate owners of Marsh Point and have been for a hundred years!"

The lieutenant sighed. "Could we stick to current history? The diary, Mr. Harling. You say it was never missing?"

"That's right. I only claimed it was gone to keep my nephew on the case. He and Miss Marsh . . . well, their relationship was about to go sour unless Winthrop did something, and I felt he was of a mind to do nothing at all, and therefore . . ."

Hannah could feel Win stiffening beside her and smiled. His uncle, she thought, was every bit as exasperating as her cousin. "I wouldn't," he said, "have done nothing."

Jonathan Harling shrugged. "Couldn't take that chance, m'boy."

The lieutenant continued. "How do you know Fowler read the diary?"

"Common sense," Jonathan replied simply.

Thackeray snorted. "A damned good guess is what it was."

"If you knew the Harlings knew the Marshes had the Harling Collection," the lieutenant asked, "why didn't they come after it before now?"

"We didn't know. Anne Harling was an eccentric and . . . well, she didn't care for the Marshes. She was aware of their grudge against our family and—"

"You—meaning the Harling family—didn't take her accusations seriously," the lieutenant supplied.

The elderly Harling pursed his lips and remained silent.

Hannah noticed a ghost of a smile on Win's face and felt a rush of pure affection for him.

"But Preston Fowler did," the lieutenant went on. "What made you suspect him?"

Jonathan squirmed.

"Tell him," his nephew ordered.

The old man grimaced. "I didn't think—I didn't believe Hannah, although a Marsh, was capable of ransacking my apartment. I knew my nephew didn't do it, and I knew *I* didn't do it."

"Why not a random thief?"

"Impossible."

His tone was so supercilious and dismissive that even the lieutenant didn't argue. He muttered something about not dealing with Nero Wolfe here and proceeded with his questioning, finally sending them all home with orders to stick around, because he was sure to need further clarifications. They began to head back toward the house.

"By the way, Thackeray," the officer said to his retreating fellow townsman, "what's this about you holding a gun on Fowler? Seems to me you don't have a weapon registered."

It was Jonathan Harling who spun around and replied, "Thackeray Marsh hold a gun on anyone? Don't be absurd. That old buzzard couldn't shoot a hole through the side of a barn at fifty feet."

"But you all said . . ."

"A ruse, Lieutenant, a simple ruse."

Then Jonathan marched out, shoulders thrust back, as if he'd made perfect sense and hadn't told a huge lie. For once Thackeray didn't contradict him.

Win seized Hannah by the waist. "I just know those two are both going to live to be a hundred," he muttered.

Back at the house, Thackeray rattled around in the kitchen and emerged with cups of hot tea laced with brandy and insisted they all drink up. For once, no one argued.

"Are you certain you don't want a doctor to examine your wounds?" Jonathan Harling asked Hannah.

She shook her head. "I'll be fine, thanks."

"It's a wonder Winthrop permitted Fowler to leave the property relatively intact."

Only the darkening of Win's eyes indicated he concurred with his uncle. All things considered, he was being remarkably untalkative. He never, however, left Hannah's side.

"Winthrop, hell," she said spiritedly. "It's a wonder *I* let him leave intact. Did he hurt you at all, Cousin Thackeray?"

"Only my pride. I have never done anything so difficult as leaving you in the clutches of that man, but I knew he had a gun, and I would be of no use to you, dead or maimed." He swirled around a mouthful of tea and then swallowed; gradually his face regained its color. "He sneaked into the house while Win and Jonathan were off plotting. You had gone, and I'm afraid he took me quite by surprise. Clearly he had no idea the Harlings were about. He thought he would just have to contend with Hannah and me. Of course, we would have managed."

Jonathan Harling opened his mouth, but his nephew cut him off before he could speak. "I'm glad things worked out."

"I just have one more question," Hannah said, her gaze taking in both old men. "You two were at Harvard together?"

Thackeray's face took on a look of pure distaste and Jonathan's matched it.

"Cousin Thackeray, you never told me you attended Harvard!"

"I'm not proud of it," he stated.

"He graduated magna cum laude," Jonathan Harling added. "Damned near killed my father, having a Marsh outdo a Harling, but I wasn't much of a student in those days. I reached my potential later, in graduate school. Thackeray had gone back to Maine by then, intent on being a Marsh."

Thackeray nodded. "Jonathan and I should have been great friends."

"And were for a while," his former classmate reminisced wistfully. He grabbed the brandy and splashed more into Thackeray's teacup, then into his own. "To our lost youth, my friend."

They drank up.

Win leaned toward Hannah and whispered, "Don't believe any of this. Uncle Jonathan's just leading up to demanding what in hell your cousin's done with the Harling Collection."

Sure enough, a few minutes later, Jonathan Harling leaned back, looking smug and content. "So, Thackeray, where have you had my family's papers hidden all these years?"

WIN FILLED HANNAH'S TUB with water as hot as he thought she could stand it and added white bath salts from a glass bottle. He had piled two fluffy white towels on the edge of the tub, where he sat, watching the water foam. He had abandoned Uncle Jonathan to dinner with Thackeray Marsh. The two would, no doubt, argue about the Harling Collection well into the night or perhaps reminisce about their days at Harvard. One simply never knew with those two, Win had decided.

"Going to take a bath?" Hannah asked, appearing in the bathroom doorway.

He shook his head. "You are."

She half smiled. "By your order?"

"It'll be good for your bumps and bruises."

And her spirits, he hoped. Since returning to her cottage she had been uncharacteristically reticent, and her skin, though normally pale, seemed almost ghostlike now. He had left her standing in front of her picture window, staring at the sea, while he filled the tub. A gulf had opened between them. He sensed it, hated it, but didn't know what to do about it.

He turned off the water. The silence that surrounded them felt damned unbearable. He felt Hannah's luminous eyes on him. He turned to meet them. "Are you going to be all right?"

She nodded, saying nothing.

"It was a hell of a scare, Hannah, for all of us. You just got the worst of it."

She nodded again. He rose from the tub and started past her, but she touched his arm, just a whisper of her fingers. "When Fowler had me pinned down . . ." She stopped and cleared her throat. Win could see the pain in her eyes, a pain that had nothing to do with cuts and bruises. "I wanted you to come, Win. It scares me how much. I've always been so independent."

"You still are," he assured her, then gestured to the tub. "Relax for as long as you want. Call me if you need anything."

And he left.

HANNAH SOAKED IN THE TUB until her skin was as pink as a lobster's, but couldn't boil J. Winthrop Harling out of herself. The hot water swirling around her only served to remind her of how much she still wanted him.

Fatigue weighed down her eyelids, while stress and the heat of the water made her feel drained and limp, without energy or purpose. She wanted only to sleep and when she woke up, to find that her life on Marsh Point was as it had been before she'd gone to Boston. Except that it wouldn't be, couldn't be...and if it meant losing Win, she didn't want it to be the same as before. She knew that.

Such contradictions! She groaned at her own confusion and climbed out of the tub, the stiffness in her joints and muscles eased for the moment. She toweled off, pulled her terry cloth robe from the hook where she kept it and wrapped it around her. Her reflection in the steamy mirror made her wince.

"You look like hell," she muttered.

Dark circles under her eyes made them appear even wider, nervous, afraid. Her skin looked splotchy and unnatural. Her mouth was raw from biting her lips. The bruises and cuts on her wrists had turned ugly shades of red and purple. She looked done in, as if the impact of what had happened earlier today had finally hit her squarely between the eyes.

And yet that was only a part of it.

The rest of what had hit her, she knew, was the impact of being in love with Win Harling . . . and of knowing she had no choice but to tell him to take himself and his uncle and head back to Boston, where they belonged.

WIN LISTENED to Hannah's request without interrupting. She had emerged from the bathroom in a robe that was surprisingly sexy and feminine, given her penchant for androgynous flannel nightshirts. "I know I look like hell," she'd said. That was the first inaccuracy he'd heard from her lips. Others followed.

But he let her talk.

Finally she finished and looked at him expectantly. He knew what he was supposed to say. Yes, she was absolutely right. Yes, he would collect Uncle Jonathan and leave immediately. But instead he said, "Let me see if I've got this straight."

"Okay."

He moved over on the couch and made room for her. "Have a seat."

"I don't . . ."

"What are you worried about? Didn't you just say that last night was just the product of—how did you put it?"

"Adrenaline. The excitement of the moment."

"Right. Then you shouldn't be afraid of sitting next to me, should you?"

"I'm not."

He patted the spot beside him.

She flipped back her hair and sat down, as far from him as she could manage. He tried not to smile. *Adrenaline, my hind end!*

The tie on her robe had loosened, so it wasn't wrapped around her as primly and tightly as it had been. He could see the soft swell of one breast, still pink from her long, hot bath. Right now, even her feet looked sexy, designed just to torment him.

He wasn't leaving.

"Okay," he began. "You think Uncle Jonathan and I ought to leave because we belong in Boston."

"Yes."

"Does that mean we should never leave town? Never take a vacation? Nothing?"

She scowled. "It means you don't belong here."

"On Marsh Point," he concluded.

"That's right."

"And you and I. We don't belong together because I belong in Boston, I'm a Harling, I make too much money, I have a city job, and I would never live down falling in love with a Marsh."

She mumbled something that he had to make her repeat, which she did reluctantly, not meeting his eye. "I didn't say anything about falling in love with a Marsh."

"Ahh, correct. You said 'being with.' A fine distinction, don't you think?"

"No."

He leaned toward her. "Hannah, you're dead wrong on all counts."

She didn't say a word.

"I love Boston, but I didn't grow up there. I don't need to live there. I am a Harling. You're not wrong about that, but you are wrong if you think it determines my outlook toward you or anything else. I do make a great deal of money, but how much is too much? And I don't, as you implied, exist to make money. I could not make another dime my entire life and find ways to be fulfilled and happy. As for a city job... With computers, I can do my work from virtually anywhere. I just happen to prefer Boston."

Her top teeth were bearing down on her lower lip, already ragged from her ordeal with Preston Fowler. Win ran a forefinger gently over her lip, freeing it, while further tormenting himself. He shifted on the couch. Stupid to have made a fire; its heat was totally unnecessary, as far as he was concerned.

"And that last—never living down 'being with' a Marsh. Hannah, I don't give a damn what people think of who I want to be with. It's never mattered to me and doesn't now." He spoke in a low, deliberate voice. "And you know that."

"Win..."

"You know all of it."

She jumped to her feet. "I can't let you stay!"

"Fine. I'll go if you want me to go. Just tell me the real reason why."

"Can't you just leave?"

"Hannah..."

"All you have to do is get your uncle, throw your stuff into your car and drive on out of here. It's really very simple."

He got up. "Okay, if that's what you want. I'll go pack up. Can you run over and tell Uncle Jonathan to be ready to leave in fifteen minutes?"

"Sure. I mean . . ." She narrowed her eyes at him, visibly suspicious. "You're going to leave, just like that?"

"It's not just like that. It's after listening to all your crazy reasons why I should and taking you at your word. You want me out. Okay, I'm out."

He started down the hall.

"Now wait just a minute!" she blurted.

Ignoring her—and his own incipient sense of relief— he walked into the guest room, where he'd deposited his overnight bag.

She was right behind him. "But you don't believe my reasons for wanting you gone."

"That's right," he agreed, shoving things back into his bag. "I don't."

"But you're not going to insist on the truth?"

"Nope."

"Why not?"

"Because I'm not a boor."

She was stunned into a momentary silence.

"If a lady orders me out of her house," he went on, 'I go. It's the proper thing to do, you know. I don't plan o share a prison cell with Preston Fowler."

Hannah frowned.

Win resisted an urge to scoop her into his arms and carry her off. She looked so tired, so damned fragile. And yet he knew it was an illusion. Hannah Marsh was a strong and independent woman who was struggling with the fact that that strength and independence had been challenged.

"I wish I'd knocked a few of the bastard's teeth loose when I'd had the chance," he said. "You?"

Surprise flickered in her green eyes, then she gave a small smile and nodded. "More than a few."

"Damned humiliating, having to be rescued by those two old goats."

She almost laughed. "At least we got Fowler in the end."

"Yes, we did."

Then the laughter went out of her eyes, and she said softly, "It was terrifying, Win, finding him up in the attic. . . . I didn't know what he'd done to Cousin Thackeray, and then, when he tackled me . . . and touched me . . ." She inhaled. "But we got him."

"I'm not Fowler, Hannah. I'm not the enemy."

"You were," she reminded him quickly. "For a while you were, and it was fun thinking that way, but after today . . . it's just not fun anymore."

Win zipped his bag and straightened, his body rigid. "Go warn Uncle Jonathan," he said.

She started to speak, then shut her mouth, nodded and went into her bedroom to get dressed.

Cousin Thackeray's house was locked up and empty. Hannah peered through a living room window. Th only light visible was from the dying coals in the fireplace. A stiff wind gusted at her back. The contrast between the cool night air and her still-overheated skin was enough to make her shiver.

Where the hell was he?

Had Jonathan Harling gone with him?

She made a hissing sound of pure irritation through her gritted teeth and went around to all the entrances, looking for an unlocked door or a note, courteously mentioning where in blazes they'd gone.

There was nothing.

Indeed, her life had been different since the Harlings had erupted into it. Of course, that had been her doing. She had gone looking for them. It wasn't as if they had decided to hunt up the Marshes and demand Marsh Point and the Harling Collection after a hundred years. Now she was taking responsibility for her own actions.

But how could she send the two Jonathan Winthrop Harlings packing if she couldn't even find one of them?

Muttering and growling, she marched back to her cottage. On the way she noticed that Cousin Thackeray's truck was gone.

Win had set his bag by the back door in the kitchen and was scrambling some eggs, apparently unaware of her presence. She could smell toast burning. He cursed and popped it up, just shy of being ruined. Hannah observed the fit of his sweater over his broad shoulders, the place where it ended, just above his hips. She imagined his long legs intertwined with hers.

It wasn't fair, this longing for him. Making love last night had only made her want him more. Made her even more aware of him—and of herself, of her own capacity for love and desire.

Her throat tightened. She cleared it and said, "They've absconded for parts unknown."

Giving no sign of having been startled, Win looked around. "I wondered if they'd end up plotting something." He divided the eggs in the pan and dumped half onto one plate and the other half onto a second. "Jam on your toast?"

"Don't you think we should go look for them?"

He smeared butter onto the two slices of toast and put another two into the toaster. "Where would you suggest we begin our search? For all we know, they've decided to go fishing in Canada."

"They've gone after the Harling Collection," Hannah said. "You know it and I know it."

"To what end?"

"I don't know!"

"Maybe they've just gone out for lobster." He put the toast onto the plates and carried them into the living room. "Let's eat by the fire. It's always easier to endure being shot out of the saddle on a full stomach."

Hannah followed him into the living room. Except for the fact that his bag stood by the door, he didn't look like a man intending to depart anytime soon. She remained standing. "You haven't been shot out of the saddle. I've just asked you to leave."

"Then you plan to continue our relationship," he said.

"Well, yeah, I guess so."

His eyes darkened, looking as black and suspicious as the day he had run into her, outside his house. "That's not good enough, Hannah."

It wasn't. She'd known it when she'd said it. She changed the subject. "What about Cousin Thackeray and your uncle?"

"They're big boys. They can take care of themselves."

"But why didn't they tell us where they were going?"

"Maybe because it's none of our damned business."

He sat cross-legged on the floor in front of the fire, placing her plate next to him. He'd forgotten forks. Hannah went into the kitchen and got them, along with the second batch of toast, which had just popped up. It, too, was nearly burned. She slathered it with spicy pear butter and felt a sudden gnawing of hunger in her stomach. Dinner, perhaps, wasn't such a bad idea.

She took up her plate and sat at her desk chair in front of her computer. Win turned so that he was facing her instead of the fire. She groaned inwardly. Why did he have to be so damned good-looking? So rich. So successful. So *Harling*.

"You look more yourself," he said softly, the hardness gone from his eyes.

She nodded. "I'm feeling better."

"Hell of a day. If you want, I'll take a spin around the area and see if I can find your cousin and Uncle Jonathan."

"No, I'll go. I know the area."

He said nothing.

Suddenly she knew she didn't want to go alone. If she had to, she could do it. But she didn't have to. It was a choice, she thought, not a sign of dependence.

"We'll take my car," she said.

12

AS CARS WENT, Hannah's wasn't much. She explained to Win that in a rural setting high mileage, reliability and durability were more important than speed and prestige. He realized she was contrasting her car with his—in essence, her life with his. Or at least her understanding of his life. There was a difference, he thought.

They bounced along the narrow road that led from Marsh Point into town. "This is nuts," she muttered.

"So turn back."

She glanced at him; her hair seemed even paler in the darkness. "What about those two?"

"At worst, Uncle Jonathan is having Thackeray take him to the Harling Collection at gunpoint. It's far more likely they've gone into town for a drink after their ordeal today. Either way, if they had wanted us to interfere, they would have told us where they were going."

"Don't you feel responsible?"

"No."

The car slowed. Hannah gripped the wheel with both hands.

Win stretched his legs as best he could in the small vehicle. "You're not really worried, either. You're just looking for excuses, so you won't have to toss me, after all."

She shot him a look. "I am not."

"Then you still want me to head back to Boston tonight?"

"As soon as we find your uncle," she confirmed.

"Suppose he doesn't come back until morning. Suppose he and your cousin have taken off for Boston to see their old haunts in Harvard Square."

"Cousin Thackeray's not that crazy."

"Uncle Jonathan is," Win said mildly.

She braked hard, swerving onto the side of the dark road. The ocean was mere yards away. Win, however, assumed she knew what she was doing, and that whatever it was didn't include dumping him out for the seagulls to pick over.

After a few maneuvers, she had the car heading back toward Marsh Point.

"I'm not thinking straight tonight," she mumbled under her breath.

Win chose not to comment.

When they arrived back at the cottage, Win noticed that Thackeray Marsh's yellow truck stood in the driveway behind his house. He and Hannah looked at each other and sighed. "I wonder where they've been," she said, puzzled. "We were on the only road out of here."

The house's living room lights were on. Win climbed out of Hannah's car and started up the driveway without a word, assuming she would want to ease her mind and find out where the two old men had been.

She fell in beside him, not looking at him, not speaking. Watching her, Win nearly tripped over a rock. Her jaw was set . . . her eyes shining . . . everything about her was alive, focused, dynamic. The near depression, the preoccupation of earlier seemed to have vanished. And, Win thought, he hadn't even gone back to Boston yet.

As he'd suspected, he wasn't the problem.

He wondered if she'd figured that out yet.

On the stone path to Thackeray's side door, she darted past him and didn't bother knocking before bursting in.

"Ahh, the posse is back," Uncle Jonathan announced.

Hannah was having none of it. "Where were you two?"

Thackeray Marsh answered. "We took a spin out old Marsh Road. It's barely passable, but we managed."

"Thought we might see a moose," his contemporary added.

They were both seated near the fireplace, where Thackeray was poking at the coals, trying to restart the fire. Win saw that his uncle looked exhausted; he was also filthy and about as pleased with himself as his nephew had ever seen him. He doubted a moose sighting had done it.

Thackeray cursed the stubborn fire and gave up, flopping into his chair. He addressed his young cousin. "We'd have told you we were going," he said, "but didn't want to catch you . . . well, you know."

Win watched Hannah stiffen and her cheeks grow red. "I was asking Win to leave," she said starchily.

"Tonight? After what we have all been through today?" Thackeray snorted and waved a hand. "Even I wouldn't do that. Damned rude it is."

"It's okay," Win said. "She was bluffing."

"I was not bluffing!"

"Yeah, you were. You've just been slow to realize it." He smiled at her. "The perfect bluff is the one you do on impulse, when you're not sure it is a bluff or even why you're doing it."

Uncle Jonathan gave an exaggerated yawn. "Winthrop, what in hell are you talking about? Carry this woman off, will you? I'm tired. Thackeray and I have a big day tomorrow, and I need my rest. I'm not a young man anymore, you know."

Hannah threw up her hands. "These two are impossible!" she exclaimed irritably. "Carry me off, like he's some kind of Neanderthal. Moose hunting. Bluffs that aren't bluffs. Crazy Bostonians trying to kill me. Heck, I'm going to bed."

"Before you do," Thackeray said, "would you and your fellow here bring in the trunk from the back of my truck? I'm afraid Jonathan and I expended ourselves getting it into the truck in the first place. It's damned heavy."

"Set it in the kitchen," Uncle Jonathan added.

Thackeray nodded. "Yes, we'll have at it in the morning."

Hannah refused to play their game and started out without demanding an explanation, but Win didn't have her forbearance, or just hadn't reached total disgust the way she apparently had. "What trunk?" he asked.

"The one in the back of Thackeray's—"

"Uncle Jonathan . . ." Win warned.

The old man sighed. "See for yourself."

Thackeray sat forward and shook a finger at Jonathan Harling. "Now wait just a minute. We agreed to wait until morning."

"I'm not breaking our agreement. All Win has to do is look at the damned thing, and he'll recognize his name in brass letters on the front, don't you think? I sure as the devil did."

Hannah froze in the doorway.

"We'll be glad to get the trunk in," Win assured them.

He slipped his arm around Hannah's waist and urged her outside, where the wind was coming in huge gusts now. She had plenty of energy to jump up and into the truck bed, ahead of him.

Indeed, the name Harling was embossed in scarred brass lettering across the front of the trunk.

"The Harling Collection, I presume," he said.

Her luminous eyes fastened on him. "It must have been out at the old lighthouse on the other side of Marsh Point. It's been abandoned since 1900. I've never been out there because Cousin Thackeray insisted it wasn't safe."

Win decided not to mention the obvious: Uncle Jonathan was right. A Marsh had stolen the Harling family papers, just as Anne Harling had claimed in her diary of long ago.

"You know what's going to happen if we leave this thing in the kitchen," he said.

"Preston Fowler's in jail. He's no threat."

"Hannah, think about those two old men in there. Once each thinks the other's asleep, they're going to sneak downstairs and skim off whatever they don't want the other to see."

"Cousin Thackeray wouldn't—" She stopped herself, stared at the trunk, then said, "Yes, that's exactly what he'd do."

"And what do you think Uncle Jonathan was making such a big deal about getting to bed for? He never turns in before midnight. It's not even ten o'clock."

Hannah pursed her lips. "They can't be trusted with history."

So they each grabbed an end and lifted the trunk out of the truck. After that Win offered to carry it himself, but Hannah was having none of that. He grinned. "Don't trust me, do you?"

She held tight to her end of the trunk. "I do."

"But I'm a Harling."

"You can't help that. Look, it's not far to the cottage."

"Doesn't this hurt your wrist?"

"A little."

He could see in her expression that it hurt a lot "Hannah, let go."

For a few seconds she did nothing except stare at the brilliant night sky. Then she looked at him, nodded and let go. Win carried the trunk into her kitchen and set it down next to his overnight bag.

"You were the one who was bluffing," Hannah said accusingly, pointing at the bag.

"Me?"

"You never had any intention of leaving tonight."

"If you asked me to . . ."

"If I *made* you."

"I'm not a cad. If you didn't want me around, I'd have gone."

"Ha!"

He straightened, breathing hard...from carrying the heavy trunk...from watching her prance ahead of him. From wanting her. "I was just hoping I could call your bluff before you called mine."

"Well, you didn't succeed."

"Yes, I did."

"How so?"

He picked up his bag. "Say the word, Hannah." His eyes held hers. "Right now. Tell me to leave and I'll leave. No arguments. Nothing. I'll go."

"Your uncle won't leave without seeing the Harling Collection."

"This is between us. Just you and me, Hannah. I'll deal with Uncle Jonathan if I have to. What's it going to be?"

She hesitated, staring at the floor, at anything but him. For an instant, Win wondered if he'd guessed wrong, if having him around was more than she could tolerate.

"You're making excuses," he said, "so I can stay."

Then she looked at him and grinned, the devil in her eye. "You noticed?" She glided toward him, confident.

"You can stay, Win Harling, under one condition: I'm not going to let you sneak into the kitchen and have at that trunk before I do."

"How do you propose to stop me?"

"You know the saying: An Ounce of Prevention Is Worth a Pound of Cure." She slid her arms around him. "I propose that the only way for you to get to the trunk tonight is through me."

"Physically?"

She smiled. "Physically."

"TELL ME IF I HURT YOU," Win whispered, pulling her on top of him.

"You're not hurting . . . not at all."

Because of the thrashing she had received from Preston Fowler, Win was being gentle and cautious with his caresses, not that it was necessary. Hannah wanted him as much as she ever had. He stroked the curve of her hip, and she felt his maleness alive between them. The earlier fears had been dissipated by her desire for him and his for her.

They kissed, a long, slow, delicious kiss that penetrated to her soul.

"I guess," she said teasingly, "old Cotton Harling would have us both hanged."

Win laughed softly, running his fingers through her hair, his eyes locked with hers. "I'm sure he could think of a number of offenses. Do you feel guilty?"

"Nope. You?"

He answered by lifting her gently, and she knew what he wanted. Slowly, erotically, she brought him inside her.

"I don't want to hurt you," he murmured close to her, "not ever."

Then he inhaled, letting her set the pace. She did so eagerly, believing once more in her capacity to confront the future, however different it might be from the one she'd imagined for herself only a few weeks before.

DESPITE HER BEST efforts to avoid the predicament, Hannah had fallen asleep, her body mercilessly intertwined with Win's. It had been that kind of night. She woke with the first light of dawn, impatiently taking a minute to plan her escape.

Finally, carefully lifting his arm from her waist, she peeled her top half free and raised herself upon one elbow. He looked so innocent in sleep. But he was a competent man, strong-willed, caring, not one to cross. Locking the doors and pulling the shades and curtains had been his idea; he hadn't trusted their two elderly neighbors not to barge in on them.

She contemplated her next move. Somehow she had to extricate the lower half of her body. How had she got into such a position?

Then she remembered.

Oh, she remembered.

In the middle of the night she had stirred in the darkness, half-asleep, the nightmare still swirling around her . . . Preston Fowler on top of her . . . Cousin Thackay in danger. She had cried out, and Win had been there, wide-awake, pushing back the shadows, he'd said, of his own nightmare. They'd clung to each other and fallen asleep that way.

How could she go back to sleeping alone? An occasional night or two, perhaps. But not permanently. Not because she had been unhappy before she met and fell in love with J. Winthrop Harling. But because she *had* met him and fallen in love with him.

Still, there were his legs and other things between her and freedom.

She bent down and listened to his steady breathing; he was definitely asleep. Slowly, biting down now on her lower lip, she eased her left leg free, holding her breath when he flopped over and lay on his stomach. His hair brushed against her breasts. She almost groaned, wanting him all over again.

Exhaling silently, she yanked out her right leg in one quick movement. It was the only way to go. Given its delicate position, anything else would have just started things up again and then she'd have been in a mess.

She was free.

On the wrong side of the bed.

With her spectacular view of the water and solitary sleeping habits, she had pushed her bed against the wall, so that she could just open her eyes and see out the window. It was almost like sleeping outside. Now however, she was on the wall side of the bed.

Which meant crawling over her sleeping partner.

There'd be hell to pay if he caught her.

But how could she ever explain to Cousin Thackeray that she'd spent the night making love to a Har ling, instead of doing her damnedest to get the first look at the Harling Collection? If there was anything in it that would cause him to lose Marsh Point, she owed it to him to find it and keep it out of Harling hands. Her biography of Priscilla Marsh was only a secondary concern.

She raised herself and carefully lifted one knee over Win's hips, his narrowest point. Quickly she lowered one hand to his side of the bed, all the while lifting her other knee. It was a tricky maneuver. She had to roll onto her side without rocking the bed and waking him up.

She kept on rolling, right out of bed, grabbed her robe and tiptoed down the hall to the kitchen.

The trunk was gone.

Gone!

"That sneaky old goat! Wait until Cousin Thackeray finds out. He'll . . ."

"He'll what?" Win asked languidly. He was leaning against the door frame behind her.

She whirled around. "Well, good morning. I was awake and thought I'd make coffee. . . ."

"Then why the big production to get out of bed?"

"I didn't want to wake you."

"I'll bet the hell you didn't."

"Now, Win, I know what you're thinking, and I don't blame you. . . ."

"Because I'm right."

"That's not the point. The point is, where's the damned Harling Collection?"

He came into the kitchen and leaned against the counter. She had already noticed he hadn't bothered with a robe or anything else, which made his presence even more distracting.

"Aren't you cold?" she demanded.

He smiled. "On the contrary."

Evidence to that fact was becoming increasingly apparent. Then Hannah realized she hadn't bothered tying her robe and it was hanging open, revealing everything. "The Harling Collection!" she cried hoarsely. "Where is it?"

"On its way to Boston."

"Boston! Win Harling, you double-crossing bastard! You took advantage of me so I'd sleep like the dead and you and that old goat of an uncle of yours could pull a fast one on us Marshes and—"

"And do you want the real story, or do you want to rant and rave for a while?"

She shut her mouth and tied her robe. Tightly. *So there,* she thought.

Win smiled faintly. "I carted the trunk back to your cousin's truck while you were sound asleep. He and Uncle Jonathan promised to leave at the crack of dawn—which it is—to take it to the Athenaeum, where it can be catalogued by qualified, neutral historians."

"I'm a qualified historian!"

"You're not neutral."

No, she thought, *I'm not.* It was a point she knew she needed to concede. An objective biography of Priscilla Marsh had never really been possible for her, either.

"They both agreed?" she asked.

"Not without a hell of a lot of arguing."

Hannah sighed. "Will wonders never cease? Cousin Thackeray must not be too worried about the collection corroborating the Harling claim to Marsh Point."

"No, he's not."

"You sound awfully confident."

"I am." And he nodded toward a large, manila envelope on her kitchen table. "Open it."

She did so, her fingers trembling. Inside were several sheets of yellowed, near-crumbling paper.

"It's tough going," Win explained, "but basically it lays out the details of how the Marshes managed to hoodwink the Harlings out of Marsh Point. I showed it to your cousin before he left and promised I would keep it separate from the collection. You know what he said?"

"Win . . ."

"He said, 'What the devil! You know damned well you Harlings used your power and influence to get your hands on Marsh Point, just when we were set to make our purchase.' He claims whatever the Marshes did, it was not without justification. He also said—and again I quote—'We won't sort out the legal mess until after I'm dead and then Hannah will have Marsh Point and you can fight *her* for it.' And then he grinned—you know that grin of his—and suggested it'd be a hell of a fight." Win laughed. "He's an old cuss, Hannah. He wasn't worried one bit about those papers. You know why?"

She shook her head.

He came to her and undid the tie on her robe, letting it fall open before he slipped his arms around her waist.

His mouth descended to hers and he kissed her briefly, flicking his tongue against hers. "Because he knows the Marsh and Harling feud ends with us. He knows we're going to be together forever." Win lifted her to his waist, while she held onto his shoulders and let him ease her onto him, welcoming his heat. He kissed her hair, whispering, "And so do I."

"Win..."

"Just say it, Hannah."

"Forever."

A MONTH LATER the Marshes and the Harlings made headlines once more.

It seemed, the newspaper reported, that the newly recovered Harling Collection included not only a rare copy of the Declaration of Independence worth over a million dollars, but an order signed by Judge Cotton Harling in 1693, exonerating Priscilla Marsh of the charges against her. She had, the judge said he'd come to realize, only been teaching young Boston ladies traditional herbal remedies, not witchcraft. But due to some unexplained mix-up, the order had come too late to save the doomed, fair-haired Bostonian.

The copy of the Declaration of Independence, it seemed, had been authenticated, its value assured. Its ownership, however, was in dispute. Jonathan Harling claimed it belonged to his family. Thackeray Marsh claimed it belonged to his. Neither would budge.

Reached for comment, Hannah Marsh, the newly appointed, part-time director of the New England Athenaeum—Preston Fowler was awaiting trial—had suggested the two elderly Harvard-trained historians sign a joint declaration donating the document to the prestigious institution.

Both men had replied, in effect, "In a pig's eye."

J. Winthrop Harling had had no comment, except to say he was planning to whisk Hannah Marsh away on a honeymoon, to a part of the world where they were not likely to bump into anything remotely historical.

Taking a break from her biography of Priscilla, Hannah read the entertaining article aloud to Win while he stripped wallpaper from the dining room of the Harling House on Beacon Hill. His parents were driving up next weekend from New York for a visit. Hannah was anxious to meet them. She and Win had invited Cousin Thackeray down for dinner, but he'd said that'd be too many Harlings in one room for him. Old prejudices died hard.

"Did you say 'historical' in a scathing tone?" she asked her husband.

"As scathing as I could manage."

She grinned at him. Marsh Point and Beacon Hill. Maine and Boston. A Marsh and a Harling. "It's a good thing we love each other, isn't it?"

He smiled. "A very good thing."

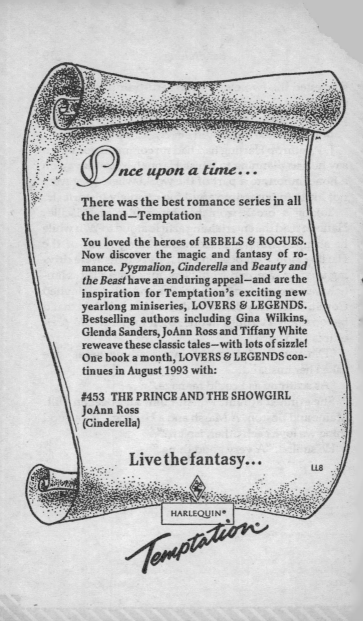

HARLEQUIN®

Temptation®

NEW AUTHOR

THE VOICES OF
TOMORROW TODAY

Sensuous, bold, sometimes controversial, Harlequin Temptation novels are stories of women today—the attitudes, desires, lives and language of the nineties.

The distinctive voices of our authors is the hallmark of Temptation. We are proud to announce two new voices are joining the spectacular Temptation lineup.

Kate Hoffman, *INDECENT EXPOSURE*, #456, August 1993

Jennifer Crusie, *MANHUNTING*, #463, October 1993

Tune in to the hottest station on the romance dial—Temptation!

HT

LIGHTS, CAMERA, ACTION!

Hollywood Dynasty

HARLEQUIN®
Temptation

The Kingstons are Hollywood—two generations of box-office legends in front of and behind the cameras. In this fast-paced world egos compete for the spotlight and intimate secrets make tabloid headlines. Gage—the cinematographer, Pierce—the actor and Claire—the producer struggle for success in an unpredictable business where a single film can make or break you.

By the time the credits roll, will they discover that the ultimate challenge is far more personal? Share the behind-the-scenes dreams and dramas in this blockbuster miniseries by Candace Schuler!

THE OTHER WOMAN, #451 (July 1993)
JUST ANOTHER PRETTY FACE, #459 (September 1993)
THE RIGHT DIRECTION, #467 (November 1993)

Coming soon to your favorite retail outlet.